FERN G. BROWN

You're Somebody Special on a Horse

Illustrated by

Frank C. Murphy

Albert Whitman & Company
Chicago

This book is for my five special somebodies:
Allison, Stacey, Marni, Cristi and Blaine.

Library of Congress Cataloging in Publication Data

Brown, Fern.
    You're somebody special on a horse.
    (A Pilot book)
    SUMMARY: Marni must lose her beloved horse to spend
more time studying, but when she helps in a program for
handicapped riders she gains new insight into her problem.
    [1. Horses—Fiction. 2. Physically handicapped—
Fiction] I. Murphy, Frank C. II. Title.
PZ7.B81356Yo   [Fic]   77-7506
ISBN 0-8075-9447-4

The author and editors wish to acknowledge with grateful thanks the assistance given us in preparing this book by the following:

Riding for the Handicapped   Robert Shearman, Executive Director of Acorn Hill Equestrian Center, Naperville, Illinois, and Judy Geise, Instructor, in the Riding for the Handicapped Program, based on standard practices presented in the training manual on therapeutic riding for the handicapped, *It Is Ability That Counts*, by Lida L. McCowen, Executive Director, Cheff Center for the Handicapped, Augusta, Michigan.

Psychological Consultant   Billie S. Lazar, Ph.D., Clinical Psychologist, Assistant Professor of Psychology in the Department of Psychiatry, Center for Handicapped Children, University of Illinois Medical Center.

Equine Matters   Tom Mick, Judge, approved by the American Quarter Horse Association, Appaloosa Horse Club, and Paint Horse Association.

Manuscript Assistance   Leonard J. Brown, Arlene Duda, Frances Lindstrom, and Marion Markham.

CONTENTS

1 A Bad Day for Marni   7
2 "I Can't Live Without Koke!"   17
3 Program for Handicapped Kids   26
4 Kevin Meets Koke   37
5 Marni Tries for a Blue Ribbon   46
6 "You Ride Like John Wayne"   57
7 Can Marni Find the Key?   67
8 Somebody Special on a Horse   80
9 Kevin's No Quitter   89
10 Big Show Today   98
11 Marni's Last Chance   112
12 The Decision   124

1

A BAD DAY FOR MARNI

MARNI BROWN'S ELBOW ached from brushing her horse in circles with the rubber currycomb. But she didn't stop until she had polished him sleek with a soft brush. Stepping back in the stable aisle, she admired her work. Koke's reddish brown coat was as smooth as Marni's velvet-covered safety helmet.

"You look super, Kokey—like a blue-ribbon winner!"

Marni had never won a first-place blue ribbon, but she daydreamed about winning. She hardly thought about anything else. That's why she spent so much time schooling Koke for horse shows. Even when she should have been doing homework. What a relief to be on summer vacation!

As Marni tapped the currycomb against her boot heel to clean it, she noticed someone approaching.

"Marni?"

It was Dayna Aslin, dressed in a beige shirt and stretch breeches like the yellow outfit Marni wore. Dayna looked worried.

"Oh, hi," Marni said. "What's up?"

"I heard you were going to take Koke over the arena jumps." Dayna knew everything that went on at Riverwoods Riding Center.

"Yep," said Marni.

"Some of the jumps are too high for juniors," Dayna warned.

Marni said, "Captain Blaine gave me permission. And he didn't say not to jump."

Dayna swept a dark strand from her forehead. "Well, I thought I'd tell you—take it easy, huh?" Dayna's boot heels clicked against the concrete as she walked out.

Marni quickly saddled and bridled Koke and led him to the mounting block in the indoor arena. Six jumps were placed in an oval pattern. They didn't seem all that high. Well, maybe the imitation brick wall. . .

Perhaps she was pushing Koke. The junior class horses weren't supposed to take senior jumps. But with the horse show only a week away, Marni needed all the practice she could get. If only she could win a blue ribbon! She had confidence in Koke. It seemed like a good idea to try him over the senior jumps.

Marni pulled on her safety helmet and buckled the chin strap. Tucking in a stray, blonde curl, she was conscious that Dayna and the others were watching in the grandstand.

She noticed one tall, skinny kid alone, leaning on the rail. Funny she'd never seen him around.

Koke waited patiently. Standing on his left, Marni placed her foot in the metal stirrup. She grabbed Koke's mane, swung the other leg over, and settled in her forward seat jumping saddle. It was flat in the center and curved slightly in front and back.

Dayna said, "Watch Marni. She's going to try it."

"Wow!" Eric Michaels exclaimed.

Let them talk, Marni thought. She leaned down and stroked Koke's strong neck. "You can do it, Kokey," she whispered into his black mane.

Koke wriggled his small ears as if he understood. He was a well-trained Morab gelding, a cross between an Arab and a Morgan. And he had a lot of horse sense.

Feeling everyone's eyes on her, Marni gathered up the reins. She squeezed her legs and signaled Koke to jog in a circle in front of the twelve-foot starting marker. The horse obeyed, then stretched out toward the first jump, a low green hedge. Koke increased his speed, went gracefully over the hedge, and cantered clockwise to the next jump.

The coop, a triangle of red wood planking, was no problem, either. Nor was the striped post and rail, although it was two inches higher than the other jumps.

But as they approached the next jump, Marni's hands moistened on the reins. The four-foot wall with loose wooden blocks on top loomed ahead, six inches higher than anything Koke had ever jumped!

Too late to stop him now. Marni bit her lip and headed him at the wall. He cantered toward the jump. When he reached it, he looked up, braced his feet, and turned sharply to the side. Caught off balance, Marni sailed over his head.

The ground rushed toward her, and she hit it hard. The sand and sawdust mixture kept the dust down, but it clogged her mouth. The taste was awful.

Marni sputtered and wiped the dirt from her mouth. Koke stood quietly, head down, looking at her. Good old Koke, she thought. He has more sense than I have. I'm glad he's okay. If anything happened to him . . .

The kids clambered into the ring and clustered around. "You all right?" someone asked.

"Koke's too inexperienced for senior jumps," Marni heard Eric say.

10

Dayna gave Marni an "I-told-you-so" look. "I'll get Captain Blaine," she offered.

Marni was on her feet. "No. I'm fine. Really." She brushed her shirt and breeches. How stupid she felt. She wished a large hole would open in the ground so Koke and she could disappear. Forcing back sudden tears, she took out a tissue and blew her nose. Her neck hurt, and the commotion was giving her a headache.

Marni's eye flicked to the skinny kid leaning on the rail. The boy laughed. That's rotten! she thought. I'd like to see *him* do better.

She walked toward Koke. Captain Blain's rule for falls was to get on again immediately, as long as you weren't hurt. Shortening the reins in her left hand, Marni reached for the stirrup with her right.

"Easy now, Koke," she said. "Easy." Swinging into the saddle, she gathered up the reins. She'd take Koke over the low jumps again.

Marni signaled for a right lead, and Koke cantered toward the green hedge. But when he reached it, she felt hesitation in his body. He didn't catch her off balance this time when he refused. Koke had reason to balk, but she couldn't allow it to become a habit. Standing him in front of the low jump, Marni smacked him on the rump with her crop. Then she turned him around and went at the jump again. She tried several times before he took it without being urged by the crop.

At last, Koke relaxed. But Marni was glum. Her time was up and she'd barely got Koke back to where he was before she began. She dismounted and led him out of the ring.

After hanging Koke's saddle and bridle on the rack in the tack room, she walked him and gave him an apple. Patting his nose Marni said, "Kokey, I don't know what I'd do without you." He pushed against her with his head, spotting her shirt. She'd clean it later.

After locking Koke in his stall, Marni glanced at the clock. She'd be late for baby-sitting. She ran across the stable yard, rubbing her neck.

The Center's director and riding instructor, Captain Blaine Parker, lived with his wife, Jennifer, next to the red barn. Their gray frame house had rain-streaked shutters that matched the barn.

When Marni rang, Jennifer came to the door buttoning a navy cardigan over a white uniform. Jennifer was a physical therapist in the children's ward of Riverwoods Hospital.

"I was getting worried, Marni," she said, her blue eyes looking concerned.

Marni felt her face flush. "Sorry I'm late, Jennifer. I was schooling Koke, and . . ."

Jennifer touched her shoulder. "I know how it is when you're with your horse. Don't fret. I'll make it to work on time."

Jennifer was understanding.

"Todd is waiting in the playroom. Cold drinks in the fridge. Captain Blaine will be home by five."

Marni ran up the staircase listening for familiar creaks on the third stair. Todd, a chubby four-year-old, sat on the floor, thumb in mouth. His wavy brown hair shaded his eyes. He brightened when he saw Marni.

"Hi," Marni said, smiling. She moved toward Todd as if to hug him, but he drew away. His moods were uncertain. Marni knew that touching him might frighten the boy.

Todd didn't speak. He hadn't spoken since his parents had died. Jennifer's sister and her husband were killed in an automobile accident when he was three. He had been adopted by the Parkers.

Marni pulled a cardboard toy box across the speckled linoleum. "Want to build a house?" she asked.

Todd took a bag of blocks from the toy chest. Dumping the red, green and yellow plastic pieces on a low table, he began building.

"That's nice," Marni said when Todd had finished. "Is this *your* house?"

Todd looked up through thick dark lashes. Marni knew that he understood. Did his lips quiver, or was it her imagination? She waited. Todd lowered his eyes and scowled. Suddenly he grabbed a toy fire truck and threw it at the house he'd built. The blocks flew in every direction.

"Todd!" Marni exclaimed. "Why did you wreck your house?" A sick feeling came over her. She was sure that Todd had almost begun to speak. She picked up the blocks and began rebuilding. Children were certainly more unpredictable than horses. She'd rather be around horses. That's why she wanted to be a veterinarian rather than a teacher.

Todd sulked and wouldn't play with the blocks

again. Marni finally got him to listen while she read aloud. When she reached for another book, he pointed to the same one. He made her read it over and over until she knew the words by heart.

The afternoon dragged on. At last she pedaled her bike home. What a day! First the fall and Koke's refusals, Dayna's "I told you so," and that tall, skinny kid laughing at her. Then Todd throwing things and making her read that dumb story a hundred times. She sighed. And the day wasn't over yet.

When Marni came into the kitchen, she saw her younger sister, Lisa, sitting at the table. Her Siamese cat, Angel, was draped around her shoulders.

"How do you like my scarf, Marni?" Lisa asked, licking some jelly from a peanut butter and jelly sandwich.

Marni laughed. "Poor Angel. What that cat puts up with!"

Angel rubbed her little face against Lisa's cheek, and Lisa buried her nose in Angel's neck. "You're just jealous, Marni, 'cause you can't wrap Koke around your shoulders."

At the ridiculous thought of wrapping a big brown horse around Marni's shoulders, the girls broke up. They laughed and laughed until suddenly Lisa sobered.

"Hey Marni, I almost forgot—dad said he wants to see you in his study the minute you come in."

"That sounds ominous, what's up?"

Lisa shrugged. "Beats me. He and mom were having one of their private discussions, with the study door closed."

"C'mon, Lisa. You must know something. What did you hear?" coaxed Marni.

"Nothing. Honestly, Marn. All they said was something about a report card."

Report card! Marni had a sinking feeling in her stomach. The final eighth-grade reports were mailed this week.

No, thought Marni. The day isn't over yet.

2

"I CAN'T LIVE WITHOUT KOKE!"

MARNI TOOK a diet drink from the refrigerator. When the door banged shut, her mother called from the study, "Marni, is that you?"

"Coming, Mom."

Marni gulped her drink so fast the ice made her teeth ache. Wiping her mouth with the back of her hand, she shivered.

"You should have done your homework," said Lisa. She never had to worry about dumb grades.

"Nobody asked you, stupid!" yelled Marni.

Angel jumped from Lisa's shoulder and darted under the table.

"Oh, look what you did!" cried Lisa. "Here kitty."

Lisa's coaxing voice followed Marni down the narrow hallway into the study.

Marni said, "Hi Dad—Mom. You wanted to see me?"

"Sit down, Marni." Dr. Brown was six feet, four inches tall. In his old letter sweater and jogging pants he looked like a basketball player. College professors were supposed to be absent-minded. But her father never forgot anything.

Marni's mother, a high-school principal, looked up from a stack of folders on her desk. "Hello, dear," she said, fingering the gold chain that held her glasses around her neck.

Marni's dad cleared his throat. "I'll come right to the point."

Her mom interrupted. "Your report card came."

"All right, Marsha," said her father. "We agreed that I was going to tell her."

Marni panicked. Tell her what?

Her father hardly ever raised his voice. Instead, he'd give Marni or Lisa his "professor" look. It was worse than shouting or yelling. When he was very angry a tiny scar over his right temple turned bright red. It was crimson now.

Dr. Brown walked to his desk near the floor-to-ceiling bookshelves. He opened the top drawer and handed her the report card.

"What have you to say about this, young lady?"

Marni's eyes were immediately drawn to the "D" in English. She'd barely passed!

Mrs. Brown said, "You didn't open an English book last term."

Marni's cheeks burned. To her mother, English was very important. She'd once written a paper titled "A Comparison Between Shakespeare's Writing Techniques in Hamlet and Macbeth."

"I got a 'B' in Science. . ." Marni began.

Her mother interrupted, "One 'B' doesn't make up for a 'D'."

Marni swallowed and stared at the sunburst-patterned rug.

"We thought that caring for a horse would teach you responsibility," Dr. Brown said. "But you're so wrapped up in Koke you forgot your first responsibility—school."

Marni felt prickles up her back.

"We've warned you many times," her father continued. "Now we've made our decision. And believe me, it hasn't been easy."

Here it comes, thought Marni.

"We know you're going to have a hard time in high school with freshman English," said her mother. "So I'm going to tutor you this summer."

"And we've decided you will have to give up your horse," her dad added.

Marni gasped. "No! I won't!"

"We'll put an ad in Sunday's paper and find a good home for Koke. Sorry, Marni. Waiting will only make it harder. He's got to go this week. We've made our decision after long and careful thought."

Marni had never heard her father's voice so stern. How could she give up her wonderful, beautiful Koke? She tried hard to keep the tears back. But they streamed down her face. "I'm nothing without him!" she sobbed. "I can't live without Koke!"

Her mother tried to put her arm around Marni's shoulder. "This is important, dear. Your whole future depends on it."

Marni shrugged away. "You'll never understand what Koke means to me!" She ran out of the room, sobbing.

Marni had a hard time sleeping that night. She sat in her rocker dry eyed until after midnight and watched the clock.

The next morning was Junior Jumping lesson day, and she had to see Koke.

When it was time, she dressed, jumped on her bicycle, and pedaled to the stable without breakfast.

Inside, she whipped around the corner, whistling her special call. A low, then a high note, repeated three times. It sounded like "bobwhite, bobwhite, bobwhite."

Koke whinnied and banged against the stall door.

20

"Oh, Kokey," said Marni throwing her arms around his neck, "they want to take you away."

She stroked his neck and talked to him. Her best friend. There was no horse like him in the whole world! How could she give him up?

Marni felt tears beginning again. But she knew that it was no use to cry. Her parents had made a decision, and they'd never change their minds. She sighed and went into the tack room.

When she returned with Koke's saddle and bridle, Dayna was in the aisle.

"Hey, Marni!" Dayna was excited. "Did you hear about the new summer program?"

"No, what?"

"It's on the bulletin board. Captain Blaine is starting a riding class for handicapped kids. He wants us to help. I'm going to. Will you?"

Marni tightened Koke's saddle girth. His loud grunting kept her from replying. Then she took the bridle from its hook, slipped the bit into Koke's mouth and the crownpiece over his ears.

"I'd like to, I really would," she said, adjusting and buckling the throat latch. Then she thought of having to give up Koke and study English with her mother this summer. "But, well, I can't."

"We need two more helpers," coaxed Dayna.

"No, sorry." She couldn't tell Dayna about Koke—not yet.

Marni finished tacking up and said, "See you inside, Dayna."

She led Koke to the ring, mounted, and adjusted the stirrups. When she squeezed his sides with her legs, he broke into a trot. Marni went around the ring several times before cantering.

Dayna came in posting a trot on Blackjack. Eric followed on Trigger Pete, a large gray, waving a greeting.

Angie Harris and Beth Price cantered their ponies so close to Blackjack's rump he put his ears back and snorted.

"Hey, guys," Dayna shouted, swiveling in her saddle, "Blackjack kicks!"

The girls pulled on their reins, keeping Nutmeg and Poco each a horse-length behind.

When the Martay brothers, David and Andrew, rode in on matching chestnut mares, the Junior Jumping Class was complete.

Marni pulled Koke down to a walk and waited for the lesson to begin.

Captain Blaine Parker arrived on Duke, a dark brown Thoroughbred.

"Good morning, class," said Captain Blaine. "Today we're going to concentrate on changing speeds at the different gaits and from gait to gait. Our goal is unity—you and your horse moving as one. Okay?"

22

Captain Blaine was square shouldered with thick sandy-colored hair. A fantastic horseman and teacher, he could be as rough as a stallion or lump-sugar sweet.

Marni followed Captain Blaine's directions for changing speeds. She took Koke from a slow trot to a fast one, from a trot to a canter, and back from a canter to a trot. Koke looked around as if to say, "How was that?"

"Nice work, Kokey." Marni leaned down and patted his neck. He gave a nicker of satisfaction.

The Junior Class had learned to jump earlier in the year by walking and trotting over bars laid on the ground. Little by little the bars were raised an inch or two at a time as the horses learned to handle jumping.

When the lesson on different gaits was over, Captain Blaine allowed the class to canter over the low jumps. Koke was moving well. He took two three-foot jumps with the brush on either side smoothly, but a bit fast. The next round was near-perfect.

Marni looked toward Captain Blaine, and he gave a tiny nod of approval. She smiled. A nod from Captain Blaine was worth a hundred words of praise from someone else.

She noticed several people watching the lesson. There was that skinny kid, hanging on the rail again!

She tossed her head and signaled Koke to jump. He did. Much too fast.

Marni bit her lip. That boy made her lose her unity with her horse. Who was he? Why was he always hanging around?

She took Koke over the course again. This time he jumped free and easy.

Captain Blaine said, "That's it for today, class. Good luck at Sunday's show."

Sunday's show! Marni dismounted, stroked Koke's satiny neck, and whispered, "Kokey, how will we ever win a blue ribbon if I have to give you up?" Shaken by the thought that they had so little time left together, she vowed to think of a way to keep Koke.

Dayna opened the exit gate for Blackjack. The horse jumped and snorted. Tossing his head, he lifted his legs and half reared.

"Ouch!" yelled Dayna. "You stepped on my foot! Beast!" She slapped his neck hard. He stood still and meekly let her lead him through the gate.

"Wow!" Marni exclaimed. "Blackjack is skittish today. How's your foot?"

Dayna sat down on a bale of hay and took off her boot. "Oh, he just grazed my big toe. Blackjack doesn't know the meaning of the word 'gentle'."

Marni looked at her beloved Koke waiting for her to take him back to his stall. Koke is so gentle, thought Marni.

Captain Blaine walked over and said, "Marni, when you get Koke squared away, will you come to my office? I'd like to talk to you."

Marni nodded. "I won't be long."

As she led Koke to his stall, she wondered what Captain Blaine wanted to talk about.

3

PROGRAM FOR HANDICAPPED KIDS

WHEN MARNI REMOVED Koke's saddle, warm steam rose from his back. As she went over him with the scraper and covered him with a cooler, she thought more about Captain Blaine. Why had he asked her to come to his office? Was it about baby-sitting with Todd?

Keeping a grip on Koke's mane, Marni pulled off his bridle and shoved the halter over his ears. After walking him in a circle to cool him, she allowed him a drink of water. When he was dry, she put him in the crossties and brushed him. She'd do a better job tomorrow. Now, she was curious about Captain Blaine.

Koke nuzzled her pocket for a treat. Before Marni could pull away, he snatched a chocolate bar she'd bought at a candy machine. He ate it, paper and all.

"Oh, Koke!" Marni said. "You'll eat anything that doesn't eat you first!"

Koke rolled his tongue around his lips the way Angel did after a good meal. Marni laughed. The horse pushed her with his nose, begging for more. "In the stall with you, boy!" She slid open the door. "I've got to leave, pronto!"

Captain Blaine's office was filled with horse magazines. Copies of *Practical Horseman* lay on the floor. When Marni came in, he said, "I'll get those magazines off the chair." He scooped up an armful and motioned to her to sit down.

Marni looked at the wall covered with photos of prize-winning hunters. A glass-enclosed case in the corner bulged with trophies that said "Riverwoods Riding Center." Marni wished that she and Koke could have their picture taken accepting a blue first-place rosette.

Captain Blaine broke into her thoughts. "You've done a good job with our little Todd, Marni. June Linn, the psychiatric social worker, reports excellent progress."

"I'm so glad! Has Todd had more tests?"

"Dr. Egel just took another series. He says he's found no physical basis, like a brain injury, for Todd's not talking. The trouble seems to be psychological."

"You mean because his parents died so suddenly?"

Captain Blaine nodded. "We're going to try twice as hard to get Todd to talk again. It will be difficult for him in school if he doesn't talk."

"I'll be very patient with him," said Marni.

"You've been extremely patient, that's why I called you in. I think you'd be great working in our handicapped riding program. Have you heard about it?"

"Dayna mentioned something."

"We need another helper and a horse. How about you and Koke?"

Koke. Marni straightened in the chair.

"I've chosen the horses carefully. They all work in our school," said Captain Blaine. "I've been watching Koke. He's the right size and well mannered. He's not skittish, is he?"

"You can shoot off a cannon and Koke won't wiggle an ear," boasted Marni.

Captain Blaine smiled. "You'll have to be sure he is comfortable with wheelchairs, crutches, and the like. . ."

"No problem."

"I'll have the veterinarian check Koke tomorrow. Report with him in the outdoor ring, Thursday at eleven. One-hour classes are scheduled for Tuesdays and Thursdays. There'll be an adult leader and two helpers for each student, sort of a team. Your team will work with Koke."

Marni jumped up. "That's super!"

"One more thing. I'll need written permission from your parents to use Koke."

Parents! Marni had been so caught up in the idea of working in the new program, she'd forgotten that after Sunday Koke would no longer be hers. But maybe now her parents would let her keep him. At least for the summer.

As Marni pedaled home, her confidence dissolved. "Whatever made me think mom and dad would change their minds?" she asked herself. "I should have told Captain Blaine the truth. Now I'll have to disappoint him."

Her mother's car was in the driveway with the hood up when Marni approached. She parked her bike and walked over.

"Hi, Mom. Something important came up. I've got to talk to you and dad. Now!"

Mrs. Brown was leaning over the motor, using a socket wrench. She looked up over her glasses. "In a few minutes, dear. I'm almost finished changing the spark plugs."

"Is dad home yet?"

"He was going to do some marketing after school.

He should be along any minute now."

Marni's mother tightened the last plug with her socket wrench and attached the black wire. After slamming the hood, she took off her glasses, and they dangled on the gold chain around her neck. Wiping her hands on her jeans, she asked, "Do I have time for a shower?"

"Please, Mom. This can't wait."

A bicycle bell sounded and Marni's father rounded the corner, his bike basket bulging with groceries. "Hi there!" he called. "I know who was playing in the mud."

Mrs. Brown dabbed her face with her sleeve. "Mighty funny. I wanted to shower, but Marni has something important to discuss."

"I'll meet you in the study. Give me a minute to put the milk in the fridge."

Lisa was in the hall eating a banana. Angel leaped to her shoulder and licked her face. "Where's everybody going?" she demanded.

Marni said, "Don't talk with your mouth full. We're meeting dad for a private talk."

"Hey, you three meet more often than the United Nations."

Mrs. Brown laughed. "We won't be long. How about helping to unpack the groceries?"

Lisa held Angel close, stroked her, and said, "C'mon, Angel. Let's not stay where we're not wanted." Angel leaped down and arched her back. Then she and Lisa stalked into the kitchen.

Marni and her mother waited in the study. It wasn't long before Dr. Brown closed the door and said, "Okay, Marni, what's the problem?"

"It's about Koke."

Her father's scar turned bright red. "We will not change our minds." It was the stern professor speaking. "Koke is going to be sold this weekend."

"Please, listen! Captain Blaine has a new summer program for handicapped riders. He wants me to help, and he chose Koke, too, because he's gentle and well mannered." Marni hated herself because tears were beginning to fill her eyes. "I wouldn't ask again about Koke, but Captain Blaine said I did so well with Todd I'd be good in this program. He needs us!"

Dr. Brown unbuttoned his blue sweater and threw it on the couch. "I don't want to discuss it. The matter's been settled."

"But, Dad, this is for the handicapped. And it's only for the summer. I'll sell him in August."

"You'll still want to be in the horse shows. . ."

Marni felt her face flush. Only two, this Sunday and the big one in August. Wiping her eyes, she pleaded, "I promise I'll study English every day. I'll memorize anything—even Macbeth!"

Her mother gave a slight smile. "Just what is this handicapped program?"

"Kids who are in a special school are coming to the Riding Center. We're going to help them learn to ride."

"Well, Marni. . ."

"I'll give Koke up when school starts! Promise!" Her mom appeared to be changing her mind. "Please! Oh, please!"

Mrs. Brown said, "I know we agreed, Hal, but what if Marni kept Koke until August? The program sounds worthwhile."

"No way. How will she have time to study, work with handicapped kids, and baby-sit?"

"I'll help her set up a schedule. But she'd better stick to it or else!"

Marni threw her arms around her mother's neck. "You're great!"

Dr. Brown's stern-professor look faded.

"Well, I guess we can try it for a couple of weeks. But remember, Marni, high school can be rough. Certain subjects aren't easy for you. Your studies will need your full attention in the fall. Koke *must* be sold by then."

When Marni kissed her father, he held her face between his hands. "You did so well in seventh grade, until we bought Koke. You've got a lot of potential, baby. Don't sell yourself short."

Marni guessed he meant the same old thing about studying and making good grades in high school, but she didn't care. She and Koke had another chance to win a blue ribbon. August was a long way off.

That evening, Marni and her mother set up her new schedule. They planned it so she could study early every morning, work with the handicapped twice a week, ride Koke, and baby-sit afternoons.

When Marni began her studies, she promised herself not to let the work mount up. She concentrated on her reading for the next few days. When she pedaled to the Riding Center for the first handicapped class, she was confident that her new schedule would work.

Dayna and Eric were in the aisle when Marni arrived.

"Hey, can we help groom Koke?" Eric asked.

"Okay," Marni said, taking her horse out of his stall. "Dayna, you comb the mane and tail, I'll curry. And Eric, when we're finished, you pick out Koke's feet with the hoof pick."

"Blackjack always fidgets when I groom him," Dayna said, pulling the comb through Koke's coarse black tail. "I'm afraid to stand behind him."

"Trigger Pete is okay," said Eric. "He loves to jump, but he'd hate to have a bunch of kids in wheelchairs around."

Marni made a wide sweep with her brush. "Koke loves people." She dropped the brush, and when she knelt to pick it up, Koke nuzzled her hair and drooled down the back of her neck. Yuk! Was it ever warm and sticky!

"Koke!" Marni straightened and gave him a little shove. She wiped her neck with a tissue. Koke had such a silly look on his face that she couldn't help hugging him.

After saddling, Marni and Dayna led Koke to the outdoor ring in front of the stable and Eric followed. Five other horses were tied to hitching posts.

Captain Blaine was making notes on a clipboard. Marni waved to Beth and Angie, members of the Junior Jumping Class. The others standing around were adults. She recognized several senior riders, talking and moving about.

"Attention!" shouted Captain Blaine. "I want to explain our new program before the students arrive."

Everyone became quiet and waited.

"We're starting with six students that my wife, Jennifer, has been helping with physical therapy. Each youngster has a doctor's okay." Captain Blaine paused and squared his broad shoulders. "Jennifer and I have taken training in riding for rehabilitation to qualify to teach this program."

There was an excited murmur of conversation. Captain Blaine waited. "Each and every student is special with specific needs. They may be scared. Your job is to build confidence. As soon as the riders strengthen their muscles and improve the mobility of their joints, they'll have better coordination and balance. It may be slow going. These students will need lots of concentration and self-discipline. You'll need patience, tons of it. Your reward? That comes when your student moves up from this class and rides as an equal with nonhandicapped riders. It's a tough goal, but realistic in most cases. Can we do it?"

"Yes!" everyone roared.

Marni heard the sound of wheels on the gravel driveway.

"The medi-bus is here," said Captain Blaine. "It's from their school."

The bus, driven by a woman, had HANDICAPPED PEOPLE written on the front.

"Hey, that bus has a hydraulic lift!" Eric exclaimed.

Marni watched a ramp being lowered. A man got out and helped a boy in a wheelchair roll down the ramp. Five other kids followed in chairs or on crutches. But Marni couldn't take her eyes off the first boy. He was the tall skinny kid who had laughed when she fell!

4

KEVIN MEETS KOKE

CAPTAIN BLAINE'S WIFE, Jennifer, walked over to the skinny kid. She wore rust riding breeches and black boots instead of her white physical therapy uniform. "How's it going, Kevin?" Jennifer asked.

He said, "I can't believe I'm really going to ride!"

"Whoa!" Jennifer laughed. "I know you're anxious to ride, but first you've got to meet the horses and helpers." She gave his shoulder a light punch and glanced at Captain Blaine's clipboard. "Let's see, who's on Kevin's team with me? Marni, Eric, come and meet Kevin."

The metal braces on Eric's teeth gleamed when he smiled and said, "Hello, Kevin."

Marni felt Kevin's gaze on her. Of all the people who could have been on that kid's team, why me? she thought. But she went to the wheelchair and said "Hi."

Kevin looked up with his crooked grin. "I've seen you around, Marni, riding your horse."

Marni felt her face flush. She knew what he was thinking. He may have said he'd seen her around, but what he really meant was that he'd seen her fall off her horse.

Captain Blaine said, "Okay, Team One." He made a check mark on his clipboard. "Now, Team Two. Dayna Aslin? Beth Price? Oh, there you are."

Dayna and Beth were teamed with Gina Pavese, an instructor from a nearby stable. Their student was a girl named Suanne who was partially paralyzed from the waist down.

After Captain Blaine had called all the names, everyone began talking at once. He shouted, "All right, people! Quiet!"

The talk died to whispers and Captain Blaine said, "Let's wheel those chairs in front of the ring. Everyone else sit on the grass."

The horses and ponies were tied to hitching posts near the road. They whinnied at the crunching sound of the wheelchairs rolling across the gravel. But none shied or reacted violently. They stayed calm even when two children on crutches came near.

Koke craned his neck, blew a long snort through his nostrils, and relaxed. Marni realized that practicing with Koke had paid off. She'd pushed a wheelchair that Jennifer kept in the tack room near him many times. After a while, he paid no more attention to the chair than he did to a bicycle. Marni had also waved a stick under his nose so he wouldn't be startled by crutches. Koke stood quietly now, alert to what was going on.

Captain Blaine said, "I've asked you students to come from school without your parents. When you've had about a dozen lessons, we'll invite them here to watch you ride." He gestured toward the horses and ponies. "These animals are used in our regular classes. They've been trained specifically for this program."

Captain Blaine untied Koke and led him over to the group by his lead strap, a long piece of leather clasped to his halter. "This is Koke. He's gentle and quiet." He patted Koke. "Koke, meet the boys and girls from Lincoln School." Captain Blaine continued talking, telling about the different parts of a horse.

Marni glanced at Kevin. His eyes never left Koke. He was intent on every word that Captain Blaine said about horse anatomy. When Captain Blaine began describing the saddle and gear, Marni only half-listened. She was still remembering Kevin's look when she fell off her horse at jumping practice. She wished she was on Dayna's team, or that she could help Jordy, the boy with only one hand. She knew she could do a good job with the younger boys and girls who would ride the ponies. Why did she have to be teamed with Kevin? Ugh!

"I know you're eager to ride, but we won't do it until next week," Captain Blaine was saying. "We want you to become familiar with the horses and helpers today. Are there any questions?"

Kevin asked, "Do we get to choose our horse?"

"You'll be assigned a horse. If you like him, fine! If you want to make a change, that's okay. We're flexible."

"Will we ever ride alone?" asked Jordy.

Marni looked at the mechanical device that replaced Jordy's left hand. He was probably wondering if he, Jordy, would ever be able to ride alone.

Captain Blaine said, "Next time, we'll start the lesson with a leader for every horse and a helper on each side. The helpers will stay until you can keep your balance without them. When you can control your horse, we'll remove the leader. You may accomplish it in a few weeks or months, or it could take a year. Each person will work at his or her own pace. Even if two of you have the same disability, you may have different problems. Does that answer your question?"

Jordy nodded.

"Okay. If there are no more questions, we'll break into teams and I'll introduce you to your horse."

There was a rustle of excitement while Captain Blaine made a notation on his clipboard. He looked up and said, "Kevin will work with Koke."

"Yea!" said Kevin. "My favorite!"

Jennifer turned to Marni and spoke in a low voice. "I've got to get Todd from my neighbor's. She has to leave for work now. Can you handle Koke for a few minutes while I'm gone?"

"Sure." Marni took Koke's lead strap.

"Walk Koke around and help Kevin to get acquainted. I'll be back in a jiffy."

Marni and Eric led Koke around the ring, then brought him near Kevin's wheelchair. "Want to pet him?" Marni asked.

Kevin gave a nervous laugh. "He's so much bigger up close."

Eric said, "It just seems that way."

Leaning forward in his chair, Kevin put out his hand. "You're a nice fella." Koke began blowing through his nostrils, and Kevin drew back. "I never touched a horse before."

"Oh, c'mon. He won't hurt you," coaxed Marni.

Kevin reached out again. This time he stroked Koke's nose. He smiled. "It feels like velvet."

Koke snorted. "Why's he making that noise?" Kevin asked.

Marni shrugged. "He probably wants a treat."

"I wish I had an apple or some sugar," said Kevin.

"Oh, that's okay. He gets plenty of treats."

Marni looked around the ring to see what the others were doing. Some were brushing their horses, others were talking in little groups.

42

"Koke likes to be fussed over. Do you want to curry him?" she asked Kevin.

Kevin looked pleased. "I'd like that!"

"I'll get the brush," said Eric.

When Eric returned, Kevin asked, "Will you help me up?"

"Sure." Eric put the brush on the wheelchair tray. Grasping Kevin's elbow, he lifted him to his feet.

Kevin wobbled, trying to steady himself. "If you keep holding my elbow, Eric," he said, "I can stand and brush."

Koke was patient while Kevin brushed his face. Then, as if tired of standing still, he bent his head and pushed against Kevin the way he often did Marni, drooling on his tee shirt.

"Watch it, Kevin!" Marni warned.

But it was too late. Koke's thrust had pushed Kevin off balance. The brush fell from his hand with a clatter, and he toppled to the floor under Koke's feet.

Kevin screamed. "He's going to kick me!"

"He won't kick," Marni said, but she realized that Kevin wasn't listening. He lay on the floor, hands over his eyes, and sobbed, "Don't let him kick me! Don't let him kick!"

Marni pulled Koke to one side. Eric rushed to help Kevin, quickly lifting him into his chair.

"Shame on you, Koke!" Marni said.

Koke hung his head as if he understood.

Jennifer ran up. "Marni, tie Koke to the hitching post." She turned to Kevin and said, "I'm sorry. I shouldn't have left you. Are you okay?"

Kevin trembled in his chair. But when he heard Jennifer's voice the fear left his face. For the first time he seemed to realize that he was safely back in his wheelchair. "I'm okay," he said.

"Koke was just playing," Marni explained to Kevin. "He bumps me like that all the time. He was just being friendly."

Marni kept her voice calm, but inside she was angry. How did Kevin have the nerve to laugh at me when he's afraid of Koke? Now he'll get Koke in trouble, she thought.

Kevin was suddenly surrounded by the others in the class—leaders, helpers and instructors. Captain Blaine broke in, "Are you all right?"

"Yep," said Kevin. He seemed confident again.

"You can work with a different horse next Tuesday, okay?" Captain Blaine flicked a glance at Marni.

She stiffened. Would Captain Blaine take Koke out of the program because of Kevin?

"I don't want a different horse," said Kevin firmly. "Koke was just trying to be friendly."

"All right then. Next lesson, you and Koke will have another chance to get acquainted."

Marni sighed with relief.

"Oh, I'll probably be taking Koke over four-foot jumps next week." Kevin grinned a maddening lopsided grin, making him seem cocky and sure of himself.

But Kevin is not sure of himself, Marni realized. He's scared to death of horses. Maybe he won't even come back for the riding lesson next week.

5

MARNI TRIES
FOR A BLUE RIBBON

THE YELLOW BUS pulled out of the gravel driveway, taking the handicapped children back to school. Only Jennifer Parker and Marni were left.

Jennifer said, "It'll be a while before we see progress, but at least it's a start." She looked at her watch. "Got to get ready for work. I'll go home and make lunch. Marni, Todd's waiting in the office."

When Todd saw Marni, he ran over and hugged her leg. He's in a happy mood, Marni thought. Todd pulled her toward the candy machine, but she patted his head and said, "Time for lunch. Let's go."

After they'd eaten, Marni and Todd started up the steps to the playroom. When they reached the third stair, Marni giggled. "Do you hear the mouse, Todd? Squeak! Squeak! I'll bet it's Mickey Mouse." Todd looked interested.

"What shall we do today?" Marni studied the speckled linoleum in the playroom. Todd seemed happier than she'd ever seen him. She couldn't let him slip into his sullen mood. If she could think of something special, Todd might speak. The thought excited her.

"Hey, Todd!" Marni grabbed his chubby hand. "I know what we'll do. Play-act!"

Todd's eyes brightened.

"How about Cinderella?" It was one of his favorite stories. She'd really clown around and keep him interested.

First, she was a sad Cinderella. "Oh, Todd. Poor me. I have to scrub and sweep, sweep and scrub, rub-a-dub. My stepsisters get all the beautiful clothes, and I have to wear these rags."

Marni strutted around with her nose in the air like an ugly stepsister. "I want to go to the ball!"

Todd didn't take his eyes off her.

Now she was the wicked stepmother. She made a grimace and pointed her finger. "Cinderella! Get back to the kitchen. You're not going to the ball!"

47

Then she was wistful Cinderella who had a fairy godmother. "Oh, godmother, is that my beautiful coach?" She whispered to Todd, "Godmother made it out of a pumpkin, you know."

When Todd gave a slight smile, Marni was delighted. She did a cartwheel and said, "Goody, here's my prince. I'm going to dance with my prince. I don't care what those silly stepsisters say." She put her thumbs in her ears, stuck out her tongue, and wriggled her fingers.

Todd burst out laughing.

It was the reaction that Marni had hoped for. She held out her arms and said, "Come dance with me, prince!"

He put his chubby hands in hers. Marni hummed as they circled the speckled linoleum. Around and around they whirled and twirled. They picked up speed. Faster. Faster! Marni panted. She had to stop humming for lack of breath. "Wheeeee!" she cried. Todd's face was flushed and his eyes shining. They swayed, teetered, and began to laugh. "We're falling!"

They fell to the floor, laughing uncontrollably. Marni threw her arms around Todd. He looked up through thick-lashed eyes. The laughter died and his lips parted. She felt him tremble. Would he speak?

Instead, a sob tore through his body and tears spilled down his cheeks. She held him close. "You're okay, Todd. I won't let anyone hurt you. Won't you talk to me? Just say my name. Say 'Marni'," she pleaded.

Todd clung to her and sobbed and sobbed. The fear in his face reminded her of Kevin when he fell under Koke's feet. Kevin and Todd are both afraid, she realized.

At last Todd stopped crying and pulled out of Marni's arms. Pressing his lips together, he withdrew to his corner. She couldn't interest him in play-acting the rest of the afternoon.

Marni's disappointment was strong, yet she was sure that she could get Todd to speak soon. She'd just have to find the key.

Marni didn't baby-sit again that week with Todd because Jennifer had a few days off from the hospital. Sunday's horse show was uppermost in Marni's mind. Her studies and the sessions with her mother were a bore. Marni hated every minute of it.

On Saturday, Captain Blaine helped her clip Koke's whiskers and the fur in his ears. He squirmed and fussed because he hated the clippers. He stood patiently to have his feet trimmed, though, and he seemed to enjoy having his hoofs painted with conditioner. Marni lived and breathed for Koke and the horse show.

Sunday morning, Marni's palms were moist on the handle bars as she biked to the stable. It's going to be hot, she thought, frowning. Heat made Koke drowsy. He might not pay attention to her commands today. Was she a good enough rider to make him stay alert? Marni hoped so. She'd paid twelve dollars in fees out of her baby-sitting money to enter three classes. She was determined to win a blue ribbon.

In the stable yard, trailers and vans were pulling in for the show. A trailer with CAUTION, HORSES lettered in red, drove up. The driver called "Hi, Len," to a man backing a palomino out of a van. The horses inside the van pawed the floor, impatient to be unloaded.

Marni went into the barn and gave her special whistle. The aisles were bustling with riders getting their mounts ready. But Koke heard her above the din and rattled the stall door. Poking his head into the aisle, he whinnied.

"Hi, Kokey-boy," Marni whispered, scratching behind his ears. She put on an apron and led Koke to the crossties. He rubbed against her shoulder with his nose.

"Don't slobber on my show jacket. I know what you want." Marni fed him a carrot and set to work with her currycomb. "Your coat is soft and shiny today," she told Koke, smoothing the skin under his mane. The vitamins she'd given him that she'd read about in the horse magazine had paid off.

Marni braided Koke's mane and tail. When she was

finished, she rubbed his nose. "You're beautiful! You could win a Mr. Horse American beauty contest—a blue ribbon for sure!

There was commotion down the aisle. It was Dayna coming through, leading Blackjack. "He's so tense," she told Marni. "I thought I'd saddle him and walk around. But he's threatening every horse with his tail."

Marni smiled. Once again she was thankful for Koke's gentle disposition.

Eric came by with Trigger Pete's bridle over his arm. "Ready?"

"Almost." Marni rubbed her boots with a rag, careful not to get polish on her breeches. When she finished, she folded her apron over the stall door. Taking off her coat, she pinned the white placard with her number, 117, on the back.

After wriggling into the coat again, Marni tightened the saddle girth and mounted. She adjusted the stirrups and rode to the entrance gate. She was second in line behind Eric.

The grandstand was filling up. Marni threw a glance toward the Riverwoods Riding Center reserved seat section and saw her mother, father, and Lisa come in.

Beth, astride Nutmeg, rode in behind Marni. Dayna came cantering up on Blackjack just as the Junior Working Hunter Class was about to begin.

Nine horses were competing over a six-jump course, mostly post and rail fences.

Angie Harris said something to Marni, but she didn't catch it because the ring steward, Matthew Fritzinger, was calling her number.

The gate opened, and Koke trotted into the ring. He felt anxious under her. In this event, open to all breeds, the horse's manner and ability were judged.

Marni had looked over the course earlier. It didn't seem too difficult. When she put Koke into a canter, he snorted, eager to jump. She circled once, shortened her reins, and turned him at the first fence. He went too high, but she took him back a bit. He settled down and sailed over the next four obstacles in good form.

Then, approaching the last fence, Koke lost his rhythm. Marni drove him on, but, at the final fence, he hesitated at the takeoff and reached for the jump to clear it.

When Marni finished, the ring announcer, Ed Krinn, said, "Let's give Number 117 a big hand!"

Marni rode through the exit gate amid loud applause. Koke hadn't done all that poorly, she thought. She might still win the trophy and blue ribbon.

But Eric's horse, Trigger Pete, had a good, clean performance with excellent form, and Marni had to settle for second place.

Her parents and Lisa pushed through the crowd in the stable area after the ribbons were presented.

"That was a pretty good round. We thought you'd win," her father shouted over the noise.

When her mother helped her pin the red ribbon to Koke's bridle, Marni sighed, "I wish it was blue!" Mrs. Brown patted her shoulder.

Lisa said, "Well, you've still got two more classes."

The sun was warming the area. Marni wiped her face with a tissue. The public address speaker blurted, "All horses for Class 22 should be in the ring now. Come on, riders! Last call!"

The following event was her class, the Junior Open Jumper. Twelve horses were entered.

Her dad said, "Do you want to mount, Marni? C'mon, I'll give you a leg up."

"Good luck, Marni!" Lisa yelled, as the Browns returned to their seats.

Marni made a last minute adjustment to the stirrups and then trotted toward the In gate. This was an eight-obstacle course. Horses were faulted if they knocked over a pole.

Koke fidgeted, anxious to get going. Marni had drawn ninth in the jumping order. She fanned herself with a program as she waited. When her number was called, she took up the reins and left the collecting area. Seeing the judge, Cindy Duda, and the timers standing together, Marni rode toward them and saluted. Then she turned Koke and broke him into a canter. She circled, and he felt strong under her. Passing through the timers, Marni headed toward the first fence.

Koke lengthened his stride and pulled at the bit. She dug in with her knees, shoving her heels down, and got set for the jump. Koke made the hurdle so smoothly she didn't feel the landing. He soared over three more fences in the same easy way.

But the fifth jump did not go so well. As Koke flew over, he clipped the top bar with his foot. The crowd groaned when the bar teetered. Marni flicked a glance over her shoulder. The red-and-white pole was on the ground.

Koke lost his stride, and came on too strong at the next fence. He's going to knock it down, too, Marni thought. Koke rapped the pole with both hind feet and it toppled. Two errors in a row!

Marni sat down on him and pulled him together. He sailed over the last two fences, but it was too late for a blue ribbon. A girl named Barbara Fordon from Winner's Circle Stable won it in the jump-off. She'd been tied with Angie Harris who took the red ribbon with Poco for second place. Marni got a green ribbon for sixth.

Only one more class—her last chance to win a blue ribbon today!

There was a strong smell of liniment in the back

stable area. Captain Blaine had rubbed down Dodson, a saddlebred gelding, and was bandaging his legs. The public address system blasted out the classes by number. It would be about fifteen minutes until the English Pleasure Class.

Marni met Eric and Dayna to talk over jumping errors. Eric said, "Wish we had instant replay, like football."

Marni laughed. "Well, at least you won a blue ribbon."

The Martay brothers trotted by, side by side, on their matched chestnuts. "Hi!" they shouted over the clop-clop of their horses' hooves.

The P.A. system came on with a hum. "The Junior English Pleasure Class is next."

In this class, Koke would be judged on his performance when Marni was instructed to walk, trot, and canter. Marni's back was wet beneath her coat. Koke, looking relaxed, was chasing flies with his tail. Marni hoped he'd be alert in the ring.

Just as she was about to enter the arena, Marni noticed a slight movement at the rail. She tensed. Oh, no—not Kevin!

Kevin gave his crooked grin and waved. Marni returned the wave without enthusiasm.

The announcer called out, "Walk your horses, please." Koke walked, trotted, and cantered on command. Several times he broke his canter, seeming hot and disinterested. When the announcer said, "The following numbers will be excused. . . ," Marni's was the second number called.

As she left the ring, Marni heard the announcer say, "All the finalists stand by at the west end."

There would be no blue ribbon today for Marni Brown. Her tears fell on Koke's black mane.

6

"YOU RIDE
LIKE JOHN WAYNE"

MARNI WIPED AWAY the tears, hoping nobody had seen them. She slid down from Koke's back and waited to hear who the winners were.

"Results of the English Pleasure Class are as follows," boomed the announcer. "First place. . ."

None of the Riverwoods people had won. Marni led Koke through the litter of torn paper cups, pieces of numbered placards, candy wrappers, crumpled programs, and empty soft-drink cans.

When she arrived at the stall area, she pulled off Koke's bridle. He looked as messy as the yard they had just walked through. Rivulets of sweat ran down his sides over black dirt patches. Loose hairs stuck out from his plaited tail. When he was unsaddled, brushed, and curried, she combed his mane and tail, and picked his feet with a hoof pick.

Marni's coat and breeches were covered with dust, her white shirt smeared where she'd wiped her hands.

She felt surrounded by chatter. Riders clustered together for the usual rehash, all saying what they should have done to win. This time Marni didn't join them. What was the use, she thought. It wasn't just the heat that affected Koke's performance. Marni knew that she was to blame, too. She hadn't won a blue ribbon, maybe she'd never win one. And in only two months she'd have to give up her beloved horse!

Tears started again, but she blinked them away and led Koke to his stall. He shoved his face into the empty feedbin.

"You're hungry, aren't you, Kokey-boy?" Marni poured two feed scoops of oats in his bin.

Koke lunged at the oats. "Silly goose!" Marni laughed in spite of herself. "You've sprayed half your feed on the floor."

She filled his water bucket, cleaned the tack and put it away.

Pedaling home, Marni's shoulders felt strained. She was bone tired. Riding and caring for Koke was a lot of work.

Knowing how tired Marni was, her mother let her sleep late the next morning. Mrs. Brown rescheduled the daily study session for the afternoon. Since the Riding Center was closed on Monday, Marni did schoolwork for the rest of the day.

Her mom quizzed her on Tuesday morning and said, "You did exceptionally well today. Thank goodness the horse show is over."

Marni winced and promised herself again that she'd keep up with her studies, perhaps she'd even get ahead in her assignments.

But now, she was anxious to go to the stable for the handicapped riding lesson. Would Kevin show up after what happened last week?

The yellow school bus rounded the bend in the gravel driveway just as Marni pedaled in. There was Kevin, seated near the window behind the woman driver. He grinned and waved a small paper bag.

A helper lifted him into his chair and rolled him down the ramp. He called, "Marni! I brought Koke an apple!"

Marni smiled. "Thanks, Kevin. Give it to him after the lesson."

Suanne followed down the ramp. She pointed to a saddlebag hung from the back handlebars of her wheelchair. In her blurred speech she said, "I've got carrots." The smaller children came next, then Jordy, who was smiling.

Captain Blaine held the lesson indoors. He said that walls gave beginners confidence, and there were fewer distractions.

Marni and Eric saddled Koke and led him around by special lead straps attached to both sides of the bit.

Koke sniffed at the other horses, wheelchairs, and crutches, then settled into a quiet walk.

Jennifer Parker introduced Minna Goldberg, an occupational therapist. She explained that Minna and she would plan the lessons and measure each student's progress.

Captain Blaine said, "All right, class. Are you ready to ride?"

"Yes!" they shouted.

"This is our mounting block." He pointed to a wooden ramp with a rail at the end. "Who wants to be first?"

To Marni's surprise, Kevin's hand went up.

"Okay, Kevin." Captain Blaine smiled and handed him a safety helmet. "Put this on and wheel up the ramp."

When Kevin had his helmet on, Eric pushed him up. Captain Blaine said, "Marni, bring your horse over."

Koke stood parallel to the ramp while Captain Blaine lifted Kevin onto his back. Jennifer strapped a canvas safety belt, called a body harness, around Kevin's waist. His eyes darted around the arena. Now he seemed afraid.

Jennifer said, "See this leather strap buckled between the two saddle ends? It's a hand-hold. Hang on to it. Good!"

While Eric led Koke, Marni and Jennifer walked

on either side of Kevin. Marni could feel the tenseness in Kevin's body as she held the back loop of the body harness. His head wobbled, and he leaned forward in the saddle.

"Can you sit up?" Jennifer asked.

Kevin straightened a little, but the fear never left his eyes.

"Hey, you look like John Wayne," Marni said, trying to tease him a little.

Kevin gave his crooked grin. "They'll probably put me in a movie as a trick rider." Just then he lost his balance and fell forward on Koke's neck.

"Relax your back muscles, Kevin," urged Jennifer. "You're riding more like a jockey now." With her hands on his chest, Jennifer pushed Kevin to an upright position. "Try to sit straighter."

"Ouch! It hurts!"

Jennifer asked, "What hurts?"

"My leg."

Kevin fell forward again.

"Want to get off?"

"No!"

"I see you're not a quitter." Jennifer smiled as she pushed Kevin upright again.

They walked around the ring clockwise while Kevin tried to sit straight. After they'd gone around the circle a few times, Kevin's back tired.

"Very good!" said Jennifer. "Now we're going to stretch your muscles with exercises. We can get more out of the muscles when they're tired and relaxed. Want to try it?"

"Okay," Kevin said.

"Put your right hand on your right hip. Then on your knee." Kevin leaned over and touched his hip and knee.

"Now see if you can reach your toe." He tried, but he couldn't reach it.

"All right," Jennifer said. "Again." This time Kevin did the toe-touch.

"Great!" cried Marni.

Jennifer said, "Now let's try the other side. Stretch those muscles. Use your hand and push!"

Kevin's tee shirt was spotted with sweat.

"C'mon. Push!"

His arm muscles trembled. He made one last effort to reach his knee and fell forward onto Koke's neck.

Jennifer helped him straighten up. "Just once more. Okay?"

Kevin put his left hand on his hip. But he couldn't do the toe-touch. After stretching until his face was red, he reached his calf.

"Hey, guy. That was good!" Eric's smile showed a mouthful of metal.

Jennifer said, "Enough for now. Next lesson we'll extend the exercises by two minutes."

Marni glanced at the five other teams circling the arena. They had all finished the exercise period. In front of her, Dayna was leading Suanne's horse. Suanne was seated on a western saddle with a pommel and high back.

"Change direction!" called Captain Blaine.

They reversed. Now Kevin's team was following Jordy. Marni noticed how straight Jordy sat in the saddle. His mechanical hand closed over the braided linen reins which had leather strips. His heels were down, and his head erect. Marni thought that in no time Jordy would be riding by himself.

When Kevin lost his balance and fell forward again, he laughed loudly. By now Marni understood that it was Kevin's way of covering up his feelings when he made a mistake. It would never bother her again that he'd laughed at her when she fell.

Jennifer said, "I think you've had enough, Kevin."

"I'm not tired," he protested. "I could ride Koke forever."

But Jennifer was firm. "You've been in the saddle twenty-five minutes. That's very good for the first lesson. We don't want you to overdo."

When Kevin was in his wheelchair again, he and Marni watched the other teams work.

Marni saw that Suanne's saddle had special stirrups. "What are those?" she asked Jennifer.

"Devonshire boot stirrups. Used by people whose legs are paralyzed, or who have foot or leg problems. The leather encloses Suanne's feet and keeps her from sliding forward," explained Jennifer.

"Say, Marni," Kevin interrupted. "Can I give Koke my apple now?"

"I've got to take off his bridle. Ask Jennifer if you can come to the stall area with me."

When Jennifer gave her okay, Kevin wheeled down the concrete aisle several feet behind Marni and Koke.

Marni removed Koke's bridle and shoved the halter

over his ears. Before she had time to tether him in the crossties, he lunged for Kevin's apple.

Kevin laughed and gave it to him. "Koke sure likes to eat."

"You'd better believe it!"

"He's neat! I was pulling for you both at the horse show last Sunday. I'm sorry you didn't win."

"Yes, I saw you." Marni remembered how she felt when Kevin waved at her. She said, "I wanted to win that class real bad. I've never won a blue ribbon. But. . ." She shrugged.

"You'll win with Koke, Marni. He's special. There's no horse like him."

"I know—and now I have to give him up!" she blurted.

"What? I don't believe it! Why?"

"Because. Well, problems with schoolwork."

"How long have you had him?"

"A year and a half. I got Koke when I was in seventh grade. Just about the time I began to get bad grades. My parents think I'll have trouble in high school because I'm with Koke too much."

"You really do have a problem, Marni," Kevin said slowly. "How long can you keep him?"

"August."

"That's less than two months."

Marni nodded. "And I need him if I'm ever going to win a blue ribbon."

"I need Koke, too. Last night I dreamed about riding him across the arena alone."

Marni had a fleeting picture of Kevin falling forward in the saddle with three people holding him.

Kevin looked up, his eyes full of hope. "Will I be able to ride alone by August? What do you think?"

Marni loosened Koke's girth and removed his saddle.

"Well, you might. But it'll take lots and lots of work."

Kevin gave his familiar, cocky grin. "I'm not afraid of work. I'll practice my exercises a hundred times a day, even if my leg hurts." His grin widened until it covered his face.

How could Kevin possibly ride alone in less than two months? Marni didn't have the heart to tell him what she really thought: he might never be able to ride a horse without help.

7

CAN MARNI FIND THE KEY?

AFTER TEN LESSONS, Captain Blaine invited the parents of the handicapped students to the Riding Center. Marni arrived early and saw Minna, the therapist, measuring Kevin with a plastic instrument. It looked like a ruler fastened to a circle. The circle was marked with degrees, like a protractor.

"What's that?" Marni asked.

"An all-day sucker!" joked Kevin. He was lying on his back on a floor mat.

It does look like a large lollipop, thought Marni.

The therapist laughed. "I'm measuring the range of movement in Kevin's joints, before and after riding."

"Oh," Marni said, "so that's how you know if his muscles are improving."

Kevin wriggled on the mat. "I can't wait to show my parents how I ride. They'll be here soon."

Marni glanced at the clock. "I'd better get Koke. See you later."

Just as Marni led her horse to the crossties, Eric came into the stall area, eating a doughnut. Koke thrust his head against Eric's shoulder, pushed hard, and Eric dropped the doughnut.

"Koke!" Eric looked at the specks of hay and dirt that clung to the chocolate and said, "Here, take it. You sure know how to get what you want."

In the crossties, Koke moved his head up and down as if to say "thank you." Then he switched his tail at the flies and stamped. Marni sprayed him with insect repellent.

Dayna called down the aisle, "Hey, guys, I've got something to tell you!"

Eric muttered, "Here comes the eleven-o'clock news."

Dayna ignored him. "Captain Blaine is going to take movies of our class going over bigger jumps."

"Not me," Marni said, ducking under Koke's head to pick up his hoof.

"You hardly jump at all now," Dayna said. "You just practice your leads, diagonals, and turns."

"I remember Marni taking Koke over a four-foot wall," Eric said.

Marni brought Koke's saddle from the tack room.

"I'll take Koke over big jumps when Captain Blaine says I'm ready."

Dayna said, "You've sure changed, Marni."

Marni answered, "I'm trying to change. Captain Blaine always says, 'It's not the horse, it's the rider.' If I'm ever going to win a blue ribbon, I've got to work." She tightened Koke's girth and then led him into the arena, while Dayna and Eric followed.

Kevin's parents and the parents of the other students were sitting on wooden chairs behind a glass enclosure. A handyman unloaded the mounting ramp from a tractor. Then he set up a row of four white poles on stands about ten feet apart.

When Kevin was mounted, he did his exercises with jerky movements. He's excited because his parents are watching, Marni thought.

"Settle down, Kevin," urged Jennifer.

Kevin had no fear now. He could name the parts of a horse backwards. He knew all about currying and saddling. But although he had done his exercises faithfully, Marni knew that his balance hadn't improved.

Now Kevin went through his exercises with both hands. "Better!" Eric complimented. "Quicker, too!" He was leading Koke, while Marni and Jennifer walked on either side of Kevin.

Kevin looked toward the glass enclosure and grinned. Each time he circled, his parents waved.

"We're turning left now, Kevin," reminded Jennifer. "Pull on your left rein."

Kevin nodded, but he wasn't ready. The turn caught him struggling for balance. He let go of the hand-hold and fell forward over Koke's neck. When he and the saddle slid toward Marni, Kevin panicked. "I'm falling!" he shouted.

"Your feet are out of the stirrups!" Marni cried.

Jennifer took command. "Hang on to Koke's mane."

Kevin groped for the black mane and hung on.

Marni knew that Kevin musn't fall, and that she was responsible for his safety. Gripping his shoulders with both hands, she held him.

At last Jennifer was at her side. Together they pushed Kevin and the saddle into place, and Jennifer placed his feet in the stirrups. "You all right?"

"Sure." Kevin laughed loudly.

Marni took a deep breath. She felt as if she had been kicked in the chest.

The next time they circled the arena, Kevin didn't look toward the glass enclosure.

Jennifer told Kevin to rest. His team stopped in the center of the ring and watched Jordy.

Jordy rode without a leader. In and out of the white poles he went, making neat turns. When he finished, everyone applauded.

Suanne followed him. She held the reins, her back

fairly straight in her special saddle. Her team led her between the poles at a trot. She's looking good today, Marni thought.

Dayna called, "Beautiful, Suanne!" Suanne's face lit up with pride.

The smaller children on the ponies trotted behind Suanne, raising a lot of dust.

"Can I ride between the poles?" Kevin asked Jennifer.

"All right. But you've got to use your back muscles."

Kevin nodded, and commanded, "Walk on, Koke." His team helped him weave in and out of the poles at a slow walk.

"Can you sit straighter?" Jennifer asked.

"I'm trying."

"Hold the reins with your thumb on top. Bring your body this way." She pulled him upright and ran her finger down his spine. "That's very good! Now you stop Koke."

Kevin pulled the reins. "Whoa! Stop, horse!"

Jennifer smiled. "Catch your breath. Then we'll pick up the pace just a hair."

Kevin threw out his chest and pulled himself up as straight as he could. They went in and out of the poles a little faster. At last Captain Blaine called, "Time's up."

Marni wiped her forehead. She was warm, and her

legs hurt from trotting in and out of the poles with the horse. There was dust everywhere. She sneezed.

The therapist measured Kevin when he dismounted. He had increased the range of movement in several joints by five degrees, which was good. But in other joints the range of movement hadn't changed.

Captain Blaine held a short meeting with the parents. He said, "I hope you enjoyed seeing your children ride."

There was loud applause.

"I've got good news. Our big horse show, which will take place in three weeks, will be a benefit for our handicapped program."

The parents exchanged happy looks.

Kevin said, "That's the greatest!"

Captain Blaine went on, "All money after expenses will go toward buying horses, specialized tack, and insurance, and for training people to work in this program. And we're going to have a special class in the show for handicapped riders."

Kevin's eyes were glued on Captain Blaine as he continued, "I hope all you riders will enter. There'll be prizes and ribbons."

Marni could guess what was going on in Kevin's mind. He probably pictured himself at the big show galloping Koke across the arena. After what had happened today, Kevin needed a miracle.

When Marni schooled Koke later that afternoon, Kevin's face haunted her. She kept seeing his determined look as he tried over and over to get his balance. She hoped he'd get his wish.

Marni worked Koke on the flat and went over the basics again. She was as determined as Kevin. She wanted her wish to come true, too. Toward the end of practice, she took Koke over a few crossbars and small jumps. Captain Blaine was watching.

"You've come a long way this month, Marni," he said. "You're ready for bigger jumps now."

Her work had paid off.

"I've set up a course outside, along the fence. Two-and-a-half and three-foot jumps. Look it over."

"Okay," Marni said, smiling.

Captain Blaine said, "I'm going to take movies of your class today. You'll be first, because Jennifer had to leave early. Todd's waiting for you in the office."

Marni rode into the outdoor ring. First, she walked Koke back and forth around the eight-obstacle course. Then, after trotting a while, she put him in turns, circles, and figure eights at a canter.

"Ready now, Marni?" called Captain Blaine. "Everyone else clear the course."

Marni applied pressure with her calf, her weight swung forward, and Koke took off. She concentrated on jumping, blotting the whir of the movie camera from her mind.

Koke's little ears stretched forward when he saw the first obstacle, a white picket fence. He pulled at the bit, bunched up the muscles of his hindquarters, and leaped over it. Marni went up on his neck, her hands light but firm on the reins. He landed smoothly and then continued easily around the rest of the course at a canter.

"Okay, Marni," called Captain Blaine. "Ready, Dayna?"

Blackjack was his usual snorting, head-tossing self. He raced at the first fence, hurling himself in the air. When he landed, Dayna, who was too far forward, scrambled to regain her seat.

Marni would have liked to watch the others, but Todd was waiting. She dismounted and tethered Koke near the office. Opening the door, she called, "Todd?"

He was sitting on the floor eating potato chips from a plastic bag. When he saw Marni, he jumped up and ran to her. She hugged him. He let her hug him often these days. His happy moods were more frequent. Marni often tried to search her mind for the key that would unlock Todd's speech.

Now she said to him, "I've got to put Koke in his stall. Want to help?"

Marni untied Koke. When he was free, he snorted and thrust his nose toward Todd. Marni smiled. "Koke wants potato chips."

Todd gave her a few chips and she fed them to her horse. "Thank you for sharing."

Koke extended his neck, begging for more.

"Oh, no! You'll eat up all Todd's potato chips!"

Koke hung his head at Marni's sharp tone.

Marni laughed. "Koke's only play-acting. He's pretending he's sorry, but he's not. Say, Todd, if you stand this close and hold your bag like that. . ."

Before Marni's warning was out of her mouth, Koke's big yellow teeth were chomping Todd's snack. It didn't seem to matter that the potato chips were still in the bag.

Koke licked the salt from his lips.

Marni winked at Todd and giggled. "Don't say I didn't warn you. But I'll buy you another bag when I put him in his stall."

Koke put his head down near Todd, as he did with the little kids in the wheelchairs.

"You've made a friend," said Marni. Todd gave a shy smile.

Once before Captain Blaine and Jennifer had put him on a pony. Todd had screamed and kicked and they had decided that he didn't like horses.

But he seemed to like Koke. When Koke nuzzled his face and nickered, Todd's brown eyes were big with excitement. With trembling fingers he reached up, hesitated, then patted Koke's nose.

Marni was delighted. And she felt like cheering

aloud when she saw Todd suddenly throw his chubby arms around Koke's neck and hug him!

She remembered Captain Blaine saying that many times kids relate better to animals than to people. She thought of Kevin and the other kids in the wheelchairs. They trusted the horses and ponies. In a way, Todd was handicapped, too.

Then it struck her. Maybe Koke was the key she'd been searching for to unlock Todd's speech!

And this was the moment to push the advantage. What should she do? She had to think fast. If she made the wrong move, he'd go back to being that unhappy little boy with his thumb in his mouth.

Marni made a quick decision when she saw Dayna and Blackjack approaching. She knew it was risky, but her experience with Kevin gave her confidence.

She climbed into the saddle. "Say, Dayna," she asked, her voice shaky, "will you give Todd a leg up, please?"

Dayna looked surprised. "Sure."

Marni held out her arms and said, "Todd, come ride with Marni."

Todd looked up through his thick dark lashes. Did he trust her? The smile left his face and he bit his lip.

Oh, please, don't let his mood change. Marni pleaded silently.

"Todd, Marni will hold you very tight. We'll ride together like Cinderella and the prince! Won't you please climb on the mounting block? Dayna will help you up here.''

Dayna stepped toward him. For once, she didn't say anything.

Todd drew back, and Marni thought he was going to cry. But he looked at Marni's outstretched arms and climbed up the mounting block. Although his lips quivered, he didn't cry.

Dayna lifted him into the saddle in front of Marni. Marni put her arms around him and held him close.

"Thanks, Dayna." She motioned for Dayna to leave. Dayna led Blackjack away, but she kept looking back over her shoulder.

Marni felt a familiar tremble in Todd's body.

"Trust Koke and me," she said quietly. "We're your friends, Todd. We won't leave you. You don't have to be afraid anymore."

At the sound of Marni's voice, Koke swung his head around. "Doesn't Koke have the cutest ears?" She picked up the reins and they began to walk.

Todd was still trembling. But after the third time around the yard, he gave a little shiver, then a deep sigh, and wriggled back against her.

Marni's mind was spinning. She had never seen Todd so relaxed and comfortable. If only he would say something. She squeezed Koke with her knees. "We're trotting now. You're a real cowboy. Cowboy Todd!"

They went around in a circle.

Just then Captain Blaine walked up, carrying his movie camera. He looked at Todd on the horse and whistled.

"Can you take our picture riding Koke?" Marni asked.

"You bet! Otherwise, Jennifer would never believe this. How did you do it, Marni?"

Once again Koke trotted around the yard, and Captain Blaine caught it on film.

The sound of pails banging in the barn reminded Marni that it was feeding time. She was disappointed that Todd hadn't spoken. She'd try again. But now she had to feed Koke and go home.

Captain Blaine lifted Todd off.

Then, just as Marni dismounted, she heard a high-pitched child's voice say, "He's a nice pony."

She whirled around. "What did you say, Todd?"

"He's a nice pony."

He was so matter-of-fact she could hardly believe that he hadn't spoken for over a year!

Captain Blaine gathered Todd in his arms.

This time it was Marni who trembled, while tears streamed down her cheeks.

8

SOMEBODY SPECIAL
ON A HORSE

DURING THE NEXT two weeks, Marni attended Captain Blaine's riding clinic every day. He showed the movies he'd taken, pointing out each student's weak points. Marni also studied her errors in his still photos.

"Sunday's our biggest show of the year," Captain Blaine said. "You'll have stiff competition."

When Marni schooled Koke, Captain Blaine would shout, "You're too anxious. Your body is ahead of the horse." So she'd try to relax. Then he'd say, "Don't let your horse jump when he wants to. Make him wait for your signal. Do it again! Again!"

Marni enjoyed the hard work. It kept her from feeling the hurt of giving up Koke. Winning was everything.

One week before the horse show, Marni came home after riding practice feeling weary, but happy. Captain Blaine had smiled at her when she finished schooling Koke. She knew she must be improving.

Lisa came into the kitchen, drinking from a paper cup. "Hi, Marni. Amy Gordon and I made lemonade. It's ten cents a cup. Want some?"

"Okay," Marni said. There probably weren't many thirsty customers passing the house today, she thought.

Lisa looked pleased. "Our stand's in front of the garage. The money's for the handicapped riding program."

Angel rubbed against Lisa's ankle with soft mews. "Please don't make me spill this, Angel. You won't look good in lemonade," Lisa said. As the cat walked off, Lisa called, "We'll play later."

Mrs. Brown was in the driveway working on her car. Over her jeans she wore an apron that said "I hate to cook." "Hi, Marni," she said. "Oh, Lisa, Amy had to leave. She sold one more cup. Money's in the box. She'll call you later."

"Okay, Mom." Lisa poured Marni's lemonade.

When Marni paid her, Lisa counted the coins. "We've got ninety cents," she said proudly.

Marni drank the lemonade in two gulps. It could have been colder, but it was refreshing.

Lisa said, "There's only one-half cup left. I'll sell it for a nickel."

Marni dug in her pocket. "Here's another dime. That'll make a dollar."

"Thanks." Lisa poured the drink and wiped her hands on her shirt. Picking up the money box, she said, "See you." Then she called, "Angel! Here, kitty. Don't be mad. Here, girl!" The coins in the shoe box jingled as she ran.

Marni and her mother exchanged smiles. "What are you fixing, Mom?" Marni asked.

"This old car is burning oil. I'm adding a quart to the crankcase." When she'd poured the oil, her mother asked, "How'd it go today?"

"Better, I think. Captain Blaine never really says."

"You've been spending a lot of time at the Riding Center." Mrs. Brown slammed the hood of the car.

"The horse show is only a week away."

"And school starts in twelve days."

Marni felt her face flush. School again!

"You're late with your assignments."

Marni crushed her cup and threw it into the basket. "I know."

"You were doing okay until the horse show. Then. . ."

"But I've only got a few more days with Koke!"

82

"That's why I haven't mentioned it before. But I don't want you to fall too far behind. You haven't much time to cover the material your teacher outlined."

"Okay, okay! I'll do it. But please don't bug me."

The kitchen door shut. Marni's father came out looking seven feet tall in his tennis shorts and striped tee shirt. He carried a piece of white cardboard and a felt-tip pen. He said to Marni, "I thought I heard you out here. I've made a sign for the Riding Center's bulletin board. There'll be a lot of horse people at the show Sunday."

Marni stared at the big, black letters. "HORSE FOR SALE." She swallowed so hard her throat hurt.

"I put an ad in Sunday's paper, too."

Marni tried to speak, but the words wouldn't slide over the sore spot in her throat.

"I know how you feel, honey," said her father. "But there's more than one horse in the world. In a year or two, when you get the hang of studying in high school, we'll buy you another one. It's too much for you to handle now. Especially practicing for the horse shows."

Marni wasn't listening. She had shut out her dad's words after he said, "There's more than one horse in the world." Not for Marni Brown there wasn't!

Her knees were weak and she felt dizzy. "Horse for sale! Gentle Morab gelding. Five years old.

Jumper. . ." Those awful black lines scrawled on a piece of cardboard made it final. No more Marni and Koke. The end.

Marni thought this must be how it felt to be in shock—ice down your spine one minute, a flaming torch the next.

"You all right, Marni?" Her mother put an arm around Marni's shoulder. "Koke will have a good home. Promise."

They'll never, never understand about Koke and me, Marni thought. She wanted to cry, but she couldn't. Suddenly, she had to see her horse. She wanted to touch his velvety nose, hear his friendly nicker.

"Where are you going?" cried her mother. "It's almost dinner time. Marni!"

Marni didn't answer. As she pedaled out the driveway she heard her dad say, "Let her go. She'll be all right."

The stable was quiet except for the horses munching hay. Marni puckered her lips for her special whistle. But they were too dry.

She ran down the aisle, boots clicking against concrete. She had to get to Koke, to throw her arms around his silky neck.

Rounding the corner near Koke's stall, she almost fell into a wheelchair. Out of breath, she leaned against the door.

Kevin's startled voice said, "Marni!"

"What are you doing here?" she asked. She wanted to be alone with her horse.

"I came to see Koke."

"Who brought you?"

"My dad."

Kevin's voice trembled. He bit his lip and turned his face away.

He was crying! Marni hadn't noticed his red, swollen eyes before. She was sorry she'd been so abrupt. "What's the matter?" she asked.

Kevin was always joking and laughing and giving his lopsided grin. She'd never seen him like this.

"There's only six more days!" he blurted, fumbling in his pocket for a tissue. "I can't fool myself any longer."

Marni pretended not to know what Kevin was talking about. "Fool yourself?"

"I'm not going to make it. I'm not going to ride alone at the show."

Marni said, "Sure you will."

"Cut it, Marni! You don't believe that. Jordy's in a regular riding class. Suanne and the little kids ride without helpers. I still need the whole team. What's wrong with me?"

"Listen, everyone's different."

"I'm so different I can't even walk Koke across the ring."

Marni tried to think of something to say that would make Kevin feel better. She remembered Jennifer telling her about swimming. "You're good in the swimming therapy class."

"Who cares about swimming? I want to ride! Ever since I can remember I've sat in a wheelchair looking up at everybody. When you're on a horse, everybody looks up at you! You're somebody special on a horse!"

Riding meant more to Kevin than an exercise or new therapy. Marni wished she could help.

"Koke is the greatest thing that ever happened to me," said Kevin, blowing his nose. "If I can learn to ride alone, I won't have to depend on people to get places. I can exchange my weak legs for Koke's four strong ones."

"Listen, Kevin," said Marni, "I've got an idea. We've still got six days to practice. Can you get a ride to the stable?"

"Sure. Mom'll bring me."

"Good! I'll ask Captain Blaine and Jennifer if we can work alone with you every day this week. Extra practice helped me a lot. It's got to help you!"

Kevin gave his crooked smile. "Super! Do you think Captain Blaine and Jennifer will do it?"

"I'll ask them now. Be right back."

When Marni rang the bell of the gray frame house, Todd opened the door.

"Hello, Todd," she said.

"Hi, Marni," Todd said in his high-pitched voice. She tousled his hair, delighted to hear him speak.

Jennifer came to the door. "Oh, Marni, come in. I called you, but you weren't home. I wanted to tell you that we're going to give Todd riding lessons on one of the ponies. We just got the doctor's okay. We're so pleased!"

Marni said, "That's great!"

"I still can't believe that Todd's talking. It's all because of you."

"It was Koke, not me. Wasn't it Todd?"

He gave a shy smile.

"We'll never be able to thank you enough."

"Now that you've said that, Jennifer, I've got a favor to ask."

"Here I am excited and running on about Todd. What can I do for you?"

Marni asked Jennifer about extra practice sessions for Kevin.

Jennifer thought out loud. "Let's see. . .Captain Blaine is free every day at five o'clock. I'll juggle my hours at the hospital. Todd will have to come too, but that's okay. All right, Marni, we'll start tomorrow at five."

Marni smiled. "Thanks a million, Jennifer. I'm going to tell Kevin."

"One minute, Marni." Jennifer held her arm.

"Before you go, there's something I want to make clear. We'll try very hard to help Kevin. But he may not make it, no matter how much he practices."

Marni nodded. She wished Jennifer hadn't put into words exactly what she'd been thinking.

On the way back to the stall area, Marni forced all thoughts of Kevin's failing from her mind. He had to believe that he could do it, or he wouldn't succeed.

Later, after Kevin had left, Marni lingered to give Koke an extra flake of hay. "You know, Koke," she said, patting his nose, "I've learned something tonight. You and I aren't the only ones with problems."

9

KEVIN'S NO QUITTER

MARNI WAS walking Koke in the indoor arena when Kevin wheeled in the next day. His lopsided grin expanded from ear to ear.

"Hey, Ms. Brown," he called, "the lone stranger has arrived!" Marni giggled. "Hi, ho, Kevin! Awwwaaayyyyy!"

Captain Blaine and Jennifer brought Todd with them. Todd ran over and hugged Marni's leg. Smiling up at her horse, he said, "You're a good pony, Kokey."

Marni felt a warm glow when she heard Todd speak. She patted his shoulder. "How's my prince?"

"Todd, dear, you can sit over there and watch Kevin take his lesson," Jennifer said, pointing to the grandstand.

Todd climbed up to the top row.

"Ready, Kevin?" asked Captain Blaine.

"John Wayne is ready to mount," Kevin said, waving to Todd.

When Jennifer put the body harness around him, Kevin said, "Wish I didn't need this."

"Someday you won't," Jennifer said, smiling. "C'mon, buckle-up now."

Captain Blaine said, "After the warm-up, we'll review what you've learned in class, concentrating on balance."

Marni led Koke, and Jennifer walked beside him holding the leather in back of the body harness. For the first time Kevin didn't have a helper on each side.

"Call the commands, Kevin," said Captain Blaine.

Kevin held the reins and hand-hold, "Walk on, Koke," he ordered.

Jennifer said, "Good! You're sitting much straighter in the saddle."

Marni and Kevin exchanged smiles.

"Trot, Koke!" Kevin commanded. "Go in and out of the poles. . . that-a-boy!"

When they went between the white poles, the smile never left Kevin's face. They reversed, and he pulled the reins. "Halt, Koke!"

90

"Okay," said Captain Blaine. "Rest a while, then do it again. This time try to keep your left heel down."

As Marni watched, she thought that Kevin's muscles seemed much stronger. He was doing well today.

After Kevin did his exercises, he played a game he usually played in class. He rode up to a white pole and placed a rope ring, called a quoit, over it. Then he trotted to the finish line. In class, they played with partners and the first team back won the game.

"We sure were fast, Koke," Kevin said patting the horse's neck. "I wish Suanne could have seen that finish!"

Captain Blaine said, "Since your muscles are relaxed, Kevin, I want to see if you can support your-self without help. When I signal Jennifer, she'll let go of your harness."

Kevin flicked a scared glance at Marni. She gave him a look that said, "You can do it."

Captain Blaine said, "Marni will lead Koke, and Jennifer will walk beside you in case you need her. Ready?"

Kevin nodded. His face looked pinched as he said, "Walk on, Koke."

When Koke walked out, Captain Blaine said, "Release your hold, Jennifer."

Marni held her breath as Jennifer withdrew her

hand. Kevin swayed in the saddle. Biting his lip, he fought to gain his balance. Jennifer made a motion toward the harness, but Kevin pulled himself erect, and she didn't touch it.

For the first time, Kevin was sitting upright without help!

Sweat glistened on his forehead. Marni led Koke down the center of the arena, careful not to make a sudden movement and upset Kevin's balance.

"No turns, Kevin," Captain Blaine cautioned.

Just as they approached the end of the arena, a strained expression crossed Kevin's face. His cheeks flushed a bright color, and he teetered in the saddle.

Marni shouted, "Catch him!"

Jennifer grabbed his harness just as he slumped over Koke's neck.

Sweat ran down Kevin's face. He was breathing hard. Jennifer pushed him upright.

"Good work!" said Captain Blaine.

Todd applauded from the grandstand. "Hooray for Kevin!"

Kevin wiped his forehead with his sleeve. After a deep breath, he asked, "Can we try it again?"

Captain Blaine looked at his watch. "It's been thirty-five minutes. You've had enough for today."

"Can't I ride alone just once more?"

Jennifer said, "It was a good session. But don't overdo, or your muscles will ache."

Kevin said, "Okay. But I don't think I can wait until tomorrow."

The next day, Kevin asked to ride alone as soon as he arrived.

"Warm-ups and exercises first," said Captain Blaine.

Kevin was so impatient that Marni had to say, "Cool it, you're hurrying through your exercises."

Finally, Captain Blaine gave him the okay. "Guess I won't have any peace until you ride alone."

Kevin was only halfway across the arena when Marni saw the expression of pain that showed he was tired. In few seconds, he slumped forward.

Jennifer helped him up, and Captain Blaine urged, "Use your back muscles the way you did yesterday. Help the horse move."

"It seemed easier yesterday," replied Kevin.

On the next try, Kevin reached the other side. He was all smiles. "Do you think I'll ever be able to ride alone without you leading?" he asked Marni.

"Hang in there," she told him. "You're doing great. Just keep working."

Kevin made several more attempts to ride across the arena, some successful, others not. Marni could tell when he was tiring almost before Kevin himself knew. An expression of pain crossed his face, he turned red, and immediately fell forward.

Marni admired his determination. I would have

given up a long time ago, she thought.

It was Kevin's longest lesson. When he dismounted and returned to his wheelchair, he said to Marni, "You've been with me every step of the way. If I make it, it's because of you and Koke."

"What do you mean, *if* you make it? Of course you will!"

"That's what I mean," Kevin grinned. "You make me believe I can do anything!"

Marni knew that more self-confidence would help Kevin. Many times during a lesson he'd tense up instead of relaxing his muscles. That's why he didn't always make his goal. With all the excitement of a big horse show, he'd have to be very sure of himself.

On the way home that evening, Marni tried to think of ways she could help Kevin gain confidence. She hoped he'd be able to ride Koke without her leading. The next few days would be all important.

That night at dinner Marni could hardly keep her eyes open. She'd promised herself that she'd study, but now she doubted it. Her mind was on a monorail straight to Sunday's horse show.

She yawned as she scraped the dishes. Her mother said, "You told me not to bug you, Marni, and I won't. I'll give you the facts and let you decide."

Marni's face felt hot. Since she had begun the extra sessions with Kevin she hadn't done any schoolwork.

"You're at the Riding Center day and night, ignoring your study schedule. And you're too tired to think in the evening."

"I'll make up the work."

"How? You're way behind. I dread to think of what's going to happen when school starts."

"But Mom, after Sunday. . ."

"Not after Sunday! Now! What happened to your promise when we agreed to let you keep Koke for the summer?"

Marni knew she hadn't lived up to her promise. She'd become too involved at the Riding Center.

"You'll have to quit one of your activities and use the time for study. This is when every day counts. Give up the baby-sitting, schooling Koke, or the extra sessions with Kevin. Take your pick."

"But Mom. . ."

"No buts. Report to your desk tomorrow or I'll make the decision for you!"

Marni pondered her decision later in her room. How could she give up her baby-sitting job? Captain Blaine and Jennifer depended on her. Beside she needed the money. She'd been short three dollars for Sunday's horse-show fees and had borrowed the money from Lisa.

The choice was between her schooling sessions with Koke and helping Kevin. The last few days of practice before a show were the most important.

She'd worked so hard that she could almost see the first-place blue ribbon hanging on her bedroom wall next to Koke's picture. She'd never have another chance with Koke. The "For Sale" sign was going on the bulletin board on Saturday.

There was only one decision. She'd give up the extra practice with Kevin.

Then she remembered Kevin saying, "You've been with me every step of the way." Would she be letting him down? He was still shaky. They couldn't be sure whether he'd make it to the other end. But maybe Captain Blaine could get someone else to help. Eric. That was it, Eric would take her place!

There was a knock at her door. "Marni." It was her mother. "Kevin's on the phone."

Why would Kevin be calling, Marni wondered as she went to the phone.

Kevin's voice was shaking. "Marni? I feel terrible! My dad is being transferred to another city, six hundred miles away."

"Oh, no!"

"I don't want to go! I love it here and I love riding."

"When do you have to move?"

"Dad is leaving tomorrow to find us a place to live and a special school for me. Mom and I will join him as soon as we sell our house."

"I'm so sorry, Kevin!"

"I can't believe it's happening. The therapist says

that my muscles are much stronger since I began the riding lessons. And you and Koke really helped me with the extra practice. I hope I can ride alone at the horse show."

"You'll do it, Kevin. No question about it."

"Marni, you're another reason I don't want to move. I never had friends like you and Koke."

Marni winced, thinking about what she had to tell him.

"Some people never have anyone in their whole lives who believes in them. When you're there you make me think I can do it."

Marni was silent.

"I'm going to work very hard the next few days," Kevin continued. "With you beside me, I've got to make it!"

"Don't worry," said Marni. "I'll be there."

She couldn't let Kevin down now, even if she never won a blue ribbon.

10

BIG SHOW TODAY

MARNI WAS at the Riding Center at dawn on Sunday. But she wasn't the first. More vans and horse trailers than she'd ever seen were driving in. Several were already parked along the white fence in back. Captain Blaine was right. There would be plenty of competition at this show.

The horses were restless in their rigs. A golden palomino's whinny to a friend in another van began a noisy equine chorus. Marni stopped to watch a man unload a handsome chestnut Thoroughbred. The animal sidestepped, snorted, and almost toppled his owner.

A breeze, cool for August, swept over the yard. It's a good omen, Marni thought. The heat had affected Koke's performance at the June show. Today he'd be alert and at his best.

A large canvas tent had been erected near the main building. The sign over its entrance said "Welcome Exhibitors to Riverwoods Riding Center's Annual Open Horse Show."

The words made Marni quiver in anticipation. She was entered in the same three classes as the June show. But she had to win a blue ribbon this time. It was her last chance!

As Marni walked toward the barn, she felt a chill. She'd worked up a case of nerves about Kevin's performance as well as her own. Yesterday, Kevin had held the reins without anyone leading, but he'd lost his balance before he was halfway across the arena. She hoped with all her heart that he'd make it this afternoon.

The warm smells of hay, leather, and manure welcomed Marni inside the door. She shut her eyes when she passed the bulletin board so she wouldn't see the sign that said "Horse for Sale."

The air was thick with tension. People were grooming their mounts, shining their tack, slamming trunk lids. Marni gave her special whistle, and Koke nickered a welcome. When she came near, he blew a long snort through his nostrils.

"Hey, Koke! How's my boy?" Marni patted his nose. The horse rattled the stall door. "Wait a sec," she said. "I'll get my apron."

When she led Koke out of his stall, he pushed her with his head. "Oh, Koke, you aren't even interested in the show. Do you think of anything beside eating?"

As if to answer her question, he nuzzled the pocket of her apron. "Okay, I'll give you an apple. Now mind your manners and don't drool!"

Marni tethered Koke in the aisle. As she worked with her currycomb, he nickered and begged for more. She laughed. "Okay. Just one carrot. Our class is very early. You know you can't have oats before a jumping event."

Dayna came over. "Hi, Marni. This is the big day!"

Marni said, "I can hardly wait for our class."

Dayna sighed. "Blackjack is full of spirit today. I'm taking him out to the practice arena so he can run off some steam."

When Dayna left, Angie Harris stopped by carrying a red-and-white stable sheet. "Marni, have you seen my currycomb?"

Marni shook her head. "No, but you can use mine in a few minutes."

"I'm so nervous. I may have left it in the tack room. I'll come back if I don't find it."

Marni was braiding Koke's tail when she heard a familiar voice behind her. "Hi, there."

"Oh, Kevin. I didn't hear you wheel down."

"Who can hear anything in all this commotion? Marni, I had to see you and Koke. I'm so excited, I think I'm going to throw up!"

Marni said, "I feel shaky inside, too."

"How can I wait until one o'clock for my class?"

"Cool it, Kevin. Just cool it, or your muscles will be tense."

"Okay, coach. But do you think I'm going to make it?"

"Of course. Here, take this brush and work on Koke's legs. It'll keep your mind occupied."

Kevin leaned down and ran the soft brush over Koke's lower legs. "He's not jumpy, like me," Kevin said. "Koke, you're the best horse in the whole world."

Marni stepped back to admire the glossiness of Koke's coat.

Kevin asked, "Can I give him a carrot?"

"Well, okay."

Koke gobbled the carrot and licked Kevin's hand. Kevin laughed. "He's sure got personality."

"Fat personality. If he keeps on eating, he'll look like a mare in foal."

Marni picked up Koke's forefoot and scraped out the hoof with a pick. She looked at the clock. Time to saddle.

Her heart began to hammer.

After saddling Koke, Marni went over his coat one more time with a rub rag. She dabbed at her hat with a brush and pinned her number, 224, on her coat. When she had on her hat, coat, and gloves, she and Koke posed for inspection.

"You both look like winners, Marni!" Kevin said.

Marni giggled. "You have excellent taste in horses and girls, sir! Now, I've got to get to the ring. Wish me luck!"

"I'll be at the rail cheering for you," Kevin said as he wheeled out.

Marni mounted Koke and adjusted the stirrups. The pit of her stomach felt like a stampede of wild horses as she trotted to the In gate.

She searched the walkway near the rail for Kevin. When she caught his eye, he waved and gave his crooked smile. Marni wished Kevin's class had been first. How could she concentrate until she knew whether or not Kevin would make it?

Fifteen horses were entered in the Junior Working Hunter Class. They were all bunched up near the gate. The only rider she knew was Eric. Dayna and the others from Junior Jumping hadn't entered this event.

Marni had drawn third in the jumping order. The first horse entered the ring. Marni had planned to watch him jump so she could learn from his mistakes, but her mind wandered to Kevin again. She shuddered at the thought that he might fail this afternoon in front of all the people.

Marni realized that she hadn't looked for her parents and Lisa in the grandstand. Too late now. The gate opened and the ring steward called, "Number 224."

Marni gathered up the reins and breathed deeply. Kevin gave her the victory sign, and Koke danced through the gate. She had to get Kevin out of her mind and show the judges that Koke was capable and well mannered. But Koke wouldn't settle down. Captain Blaine had often told the class that a horse reflected the rider's feelings.

Marni walked Koke in a circle. For a few seconds she couldn't remember where the course began, although she'd studied it earlier. It was trickier than the other courses. There were eight obstacles. She pulled herself together and the course came into focus.

Heart pounding, she let Koke loose at the first fence. He flew over it. Then she heard the crackle of dirt hitting the pole as he sailed over the second hurdle.

The crowd gave a murmur of excitement.

Koke took the next five hurdles in stride, but he rushed the last jump, an imitation brick wall, and hit it with his knees. Marni had been thinking about Kevin again. She should have checked and collected Koke before they reached the wall.

Until the last jump they'd done well, Marni thought. The round was almost a repeat of the June show. If nobody went clean, she could be the winner.

The crowd applauded when Marni left the ring. But, just as in the June show, her round wasn't good enough. A boy named Tommy Lauwers won the blue ribbon. Marni beat out Eric for second place.

After the ribbons were presented, Marni walked Koke to the stall area. Her mother and father came to visit. Lisa tagged along, drinking an orange drink from a paper cup.

"Koke had it made until that last wall," her dad said.

"You almost got first place, Marni," said Lisa.

Marni hung the red ribbon on the stall door. "It was my fault. Koke could have won. I didn't concentrate."

"When's your next class?" asked her mother.

As if in answer to the question, the PA system blasted, "Class Number 10, Junior English Pleasure—in the ring, please."

"That's us," said Marni.

When she brought Koke out of his stall, he dipped

his head toward Lisa and clamped his strong teeth on her cup.

Lisa let go of the cup, and the orange drink spilled down the legs of her jeans. She cried, "Koke's eating the cup!"

Marni grabbed the white plastic, but part of it broke off. Koke promptly chewed and swallowed it.

"Yuk!" said Lisa. "That horse has an iron stomach!"

"Better hurry. It's time for your class," Marni's dad said.

Her mom hugged her. "Good luck, dear."

Lisa wiped her jeans with a rag. "We'll be pulling for you!"

In the arena, Marni searched the rail for Kevin, but although she looked hard, she couldn't see him. Where could he be? Was he sick or something?

The announcer called, "Walk your horses, please!"

Marni reacted mechanically. She signaled Koke to walk, trot, and canter, and did all the required commands, but her mind was on Kevin. She hoped he hadn't given up. Marni wished this class was over. She had to find Kevin.

When her number was called for a fifth-place pink ribbon, she couldn't have cared less. She put Koke in his stall and ran down the aisle looking for Kevin.

He wasn't in the stable area.

The show broke for lunch, and exhibitors thronged the food concessions. Marni searched the exhibitors' tent, but Kevin wasn't there either.

The kids from Junior Jumping were at the hot-dog stand.

"Has anyone seen Kevin?" asked Marni.

They shook their heads.

"Hey, Marni, how about a hot dog?" called Dayna.

"No, thanks. I've got to find Kevin."

It was getting warmer. Marni took off her coat and threw it over one arm. Where could Kevin be? She'd looked everywhere. She had even asked Eric to go into the washroom and see if he was inside, being sick.

It was almost time for Kevin's class. Marni finally told herself that he'd gone home. She headed back to Koke's stall.

But she was flooded with relief when she turned the corner and saw Kevin's chair in the aisle. "Where've you been?" she asked. "I looked all over the place for you."

Kevin's face was pale. "I know."

"But it's almost time for your class."

"Marni, all those people scare me. What if I fail?"

"You've practiced for two months. You've got to give it a try."

"I don't think. . ."

"Would John Wayne chicken out?"

Kevin gave his crooked smile.

106

"C'mon. Wheel over to the arena. I'll bring Koke. You've only got fifteen minutes to exercise and warm up. Don't worry. Jennifer and I'll walk beside you, just in case."

"Okay, coach, I'll do it."

Marni sighed and led Koke to the ring.

A man drove a small tractor with a rake attached, and smoothed the arena floor. When he finished, he brought out the mounting ramp for the Handicapped Class.

Marni and the other helpers led the horses around the practice ring. Jennifer pinned Kevin's number, 165, on his coat.

Kevin said, "I'm scared."

"Listen, Kevin," said Marni, "it helps a lot if you whistle when you're nervous."

Every member of the Handicapped Class would ride alone. They were not competing. Each had his or her own goal. Kevin's goal was to walk across the arena without anyone leading his horse or holding his body harness. Later, there would be games on horseback.

After fifteen minutes of basics and exercises, the announcer boomed, "For the first time, Riverwoods Riding Center presents a special class, 'Riding for the Handicapped'."

The ring steward called, "Number 161."

"That's me!" squealed Suanne.

The announcer said, "Walk your horse, please." Suanne, sitting straight in the saddle, followed the announcer's instructions. Then she trotted her horse in and out of the white poles. It was a beautiful performance.

When Suanne had finished, the loudspeaker crackled, "Let's give Number 161 a great big hand!"

As she rode out, the vigorous applause brought a smile to Suanne's face.

The ring steward called, "Number 165 on deck!"

Marni smiled up at Kevin. "That's you! Show 'em, pardner!"

Kevin took an enormous breath and whistled a few bars of "Home on the Range."

Jennifer and Marni stood beside him. "Relax your back muscles, Kevin," said Jennifer.

The PA system boomed, "Walk your horse to the far end of the arena and touch the wall, please."

To Marni, the wall looked at least a mile away.

Kevin sat erect in the saddle, heels down as best he could. His hands held the reins, his jaw was tight.

The audience quieted, sensing the drama of the event.

Marni clenched her fists, and her nails dug into her palms. She willed Kevin's muscles to relax with all her heart as she walked beside him.

Koke walked slowly, head up, eyes alert, obeying Kevin's commands.

They made it halfway across the ring!

But Marni knew that the worst was yet to come. When Kevin's muscles tired, he always fell forward.

Koke walked along. Now they were only a few yards from the wall. Marni thought maybe Kevin wouldn't fall this time. His muscles seemed stronger.

But his muscles weren't strong enough. Kevin's back quivered, and his body began to lean.

"No!" Marni screamed inside herself. "Don't let him fail now!"

Sweat appeared on Kevin's forehead and on his

upper lip. His cheeks grew bright red and the familiar strained expression crossed his face.

Marni flashed Jennifer a look that said, "Should we grab the body harness before he falls?"

Jennifer shook her head.

Marni's heart pounded in her throat as she watched Kevin work his back muscles, desperately seeking balance. He was tired, very tired. All the while, Koke moved slowly, slowly, almost as if he were in slow motion. The gap was closing. They were coming close to the wall. Closer.

Kevin's body dropped forward a little more. With his left hand holding the reins, he reached with his right hand. But he couldn't touch the wall—yet.

"Just another inch!" urged Marni.

They were at the wall.

Marni held her breath.

The silence in the arena drew out and tightened around Kevin.

He made one last super-human effort and scraped the wall with his fingertips!

Marni's held breath escaped in a cheer. "Yea! You did it! You did it!"

A deep roar of triumph came up from the crowd. People leaped to their feet, and the arena rocked with applause, just as Kevin fell forward.

Jennifer and Marni caught his body harness and helped him sit up.

The crowd in the grandstand kept yelling and clapping.

Marni said, "John Wayne couldn't have done any better!"

And Kevin grinned the biggest, crookedest grin Marni had ever seen.

11

MARNI'S LAST CHANCE

MARNI FELT like doing a cartwheel in the middle of the arena, leaping over the white poles, shouting into the loudspeaker, "Kevin made it! Kevin made it!"

She planted a huge kiss on Koke's nose and squeezed him. She wanted to hug all of the horses, exhibitors, and spectators—everyone who shared in this fabulous happening.

The lightheaded feeling continued until a glance at the clock brought her down to earth.

Time for her last class!

As Marni tightened Koke's cinch she said to herself, "Kevin's reached his goal. Now I can concentrate on the Junior Open Jumper Class and my blue ribbon."

Dozens of horses and riders were milling around the In gate when Marni arrived. The ring steward, Bob Kaufman, went through the crowd checking names with numbers on his clipboard. "Dayna Aslin, Marni Brown, Eric Michaels, Christopher Rosalak, Tommy Lauwers. . ."

Tommy was the boy who had beat Marni in the Working Hunter Class. She caught his eye. He saluted her with his whip. Her face felt hot from the heat that rushed up.

Dayna trotted over on her horse. Red ribbons braided into Blackjack's mane flew in the air as he tossed his head and rolled the bit around in his mouth.

Dayna took a tight hold of the reins. "Wish they'd start."

Marni nodded. She'd drawn twentieth in the jumping order. Last. It would be a long wait for her. She searched for Kevin among the spectators jamming the walkway. Amid all the noise and excitement, she spied him at the rail. He waved the certificate he'd received for participating in his class. She smiled.

Marni looked over the nine-obstacle course. The four outside hurdles were to be jumped in a counter-clockwise direction starting at the right bottom corner. The fifth was in the center. After jumping the fifth hurdle, riders had to reverse direction, take the second fence again at the top right, and then jump the last three hurdles going clockwise.

The oxer, shrubbery with a rail behind it, hadn't been that close to the corner in the diagram she'd studied. All you had to do was tick the bar and it would fall. But it wasn't the bar Marni worried about. Since June, when she'd forced him over senior jumps, Koke seemed to be afraid of painted brick walls. And jump number five, in the center, was a wall with loose blocks on top.

Marni watched a dozen riders complete their rounds. So far, nothing spectacular. There had been only polite applause from the crowd.

When it was Blackjack's turn, he rushed in, ears pointed like sharp knives. He exploded over the first two jumps, and at the coop, jumped six inches higher than was necessary. He landed with such force that Dayna's hat fell off.

Sweat streamed from Blackjack as he flung himself at the rest of the hurdles. He lunged over the oxer and took a stinging blow from the pole as it toppled. Then he charged through the Out gate snorting past horses and riders. They groaned and scattered. When Dayna pulled him up and slid off, she shook her head. Marni gave her a sympathetic smile.

At last it was Marni's turn. There had been two clean rounds, Tommy's and Eric's.

The ring steward called her number, and the riders

opened a path. Marni licked dry lips. Her hands felt stiff on the reins. Nobody was going to stop her now, not Tommy, not Eric—no one. She was going to win. She wanted a blue ribbon. She had to have it!

Kevin yelled, "Show 'em, coach!"

The gate swung open, and she left the collecting area. Koke was ready, his neck arched and his head proud. Marni saluted Judge Kari Malk and the timers. Waiting for the go-ahead signal, she blessed Koke for his manners. If she had to ride Blackjack, she'd never make it.

Koke soared over the first hurdle. When he landed, she checked him, and he pulled against her hands.

At the post and rail his timing was perfect, and he held this pace for the next two fences.

The next hurdle was the brick wall. Koke's head went up as he approached it, and Marni stiffened. But he lengthened his stride and took it with his tail flying!

With the wall behind her, Marni relaxed and let Koke do the work. He sailed over the last four fences, and kicked up his heels as he cantered out of the ring. The crowd roared their appreciation.

Koke looked around at Marni as if to say "Wasn't I great?"

Marni leaned down and hugged him. "Good boy, Kokey." She slipped out of the saddle and loosened the girth.

The loudspeaker blasted, "No faults on number 224!"

Tommy, Eric, and Marni had gone clean. There would be a jump-off for first place!

Marni shared an apple and a drink of water with Koke. He drooled down the front of her coat, but she didn't care.

Two fences were being raised six inches for the jump-off. Marni led Koke around to keep him warmed up.

Dayna called, "Nice work, Marni."

"Thanks." Marni's hands were ice. The strain of waiting was getting to her.

A ring man checked the height of the fences with a tape measure and nodded to the steward who signaled the gate man.

Time for the jump-off!

Eric was the first to go. The crowd tensed as Trigger Pete went through the gate with a rush. He took the first fence in an easy canter. Eric sat forward and gave him his head for the post and rail, the coop, and the oxer.

But when Eric tried to turn his horse toward the brick wall, Trigger Pete became confused. He threw his head, crossed, and jumped the brush fence.

The crowd groaned. Trigger Pete was off the course!

A horn sounded, signaling his elimination. Eric

yanked him to a stop, turned, and trotted out of the gate.

The announcer blasted, "Number 168 has been disqualified for going off course."

Marni said, "Too bad, Eric."

He shrugged. "Well, you can't win 'em all."

Now it was up to Tommy. His horse stepped off in a smooth canter. Spock's sleek velvet-black coat shone. He took the first four fences as if they were miniatures. Then, he flew over the brick wall and the brush and gathered himself for the post and rail. He was awkward, his feet slipped under him, and he banged the bar with his hind leg.

The crowd went "Ohhhh" in disappointment as the bar hit the ground. Spock took the last two fences in stride and cantered out of the gate.

There was a lot of static over the loudspeaker, then the announcer said, "One-half fault on Number 201."

The ring steward called Marni's number. She needed a perfect round to beat Tommy. Settling herself in the saddle, she adjusted her feet in the stirrups. She gave Koke a boot, and they walked up to the gate. The faces around the ring were a blur as the gate opened.

Once again Marni saluted the timers and judges, put Koke into a canter, circled, and headed for the first hurdle.

Koke's small, alert ears swiveled when he saw the brush fence. He lengthened his stride, eager to jump. Marni dug in her knees and Koke sailed over with the ease of a parachute floating to earth.

Koke moved in long, effortless strides toward the post and rail. Marni felt her heart pounding as he reached out and soared over it. She slid her hands up his neck and collected him when he landed. Horse and rider were in rhythm.

Arching his long neck, Koke judged the next hurdle, the coop. With a strong drive of his hind-quarters, he stretched his shoulders and flashed through the air. He landed and galloped toward the brick wall with the loose blocks on top.

As Koke neared the wall, his pace slackened. Marni sucked in her breath. She pressed her heels against his sides, urging him on with her body. Still, he slowed.

Leaning forward in the saddle, she pleaded, "Don't refuse, Kokey! Don't refuse! This is our last chance!"

When they arrived at the jump, Koke gave a snort, then leaped straight into the air and over the wall. He landed on all four feet.

He cleared the remaining fences without coming near a rail and jogged out of the arena. Marni dismounted. She heard the tumultuous applause, but held her breath until a voice announced, "No faults on number 224!"

There was a short pause and then the PA boomed.

"The winner of Class 30, Junior Open Jumper is number 224, a bay gelding, owned and ridden by Miss Marni Brown."

Koke and Marni had won a blue ribbon!

But where was that soaring-over-the-rooftops feeling you should have when your dreams come true? Marni had been close to it when Kevin reached his goal. Now, she just felt a quiet sense of accomplishment. It was as though she'd gotten something back because she'd helped Kevin.

Marni would sort out her feelings later. Now, her parents and Lisa were wriggling through the crowd that lined the ring.

She threw herself at her mother and hugged her. Her father gave her a squeeze and bellowed, "That was a good go!"

Lisa blew a huge bubble with her gum and said, "You finally made it!"

When the ring was cleared for the award presentation, her dad gave her a leg up. Koke bounced into the ring, showing off.

Marni's prize was a pair of hand-woven leather reins presented by Candy Withrow, of Withrow's Saddle Shop. The ringmaster pinned the shiny blue satin rosette on Koke's bridle. "Riverwoods Horse Show" was written on it in gold letters.

"Thank you," Marni said, smiling.

Tommy won the second-place red ribbon, and Eric took the yellow. The six winners walked a victory circle around the ring. The popping flashbulbs and the loud applause didn't bother Koke. He seemed to enjoy it.

When Marni slid down from her horse, she was surrounded by kids from Junior Jumping Class.

Dayna said, "It was your best round ever!"

"You really deserved to win!" said Eric.

Angie and Beth patted her on the back, and the Martay brothers yelled their congratulations.

Marni stretched her neck to see if Kevin was still at the rail. But she couldn't see past the people around her. It would be impossible for him to get through with his wheelchair.

Dr. Brown said, "Let's go to Koke's stall. I've got something to tell you."

The crowd jostled them as Koke, Marni, and her family went to the stall area. Marni wondered what her father had to tell her. She asked him as soon as she'd tethered Koke in the aisle.

Lisa blurted, "Captain Blaine wants to buy Koke!"

Marni had removed the blue ribbon from Koke's bridle. She dropped it.

"Lisa!" her mom exclaimed. "You spoiled the surprise."

Dr. Brown said, "Good news is never spoiled. You've done a great job working with Kevin, Marni. We're proud of you. Captain Blaine wants to use Koke in the riding school, and it's okay with Mom and me."

Marni could hardly believe her good luck. Koke would stay where he belonged at Riverwoods Riding Center. She'd even get to ride him occasionally. But best of all, she wouldn't have to say goodby to her beloved horse!

Marni hugged her dad. "That's wonderful!"

Her father said, "We haven't made the deal yet. We're meeting tomorrow. Get Koke squared away, and we'll see you in the stands."

When they left, Marni patted Koke's nose and said, "Did you hear the great news, Kokey? We're going to stay together." He gobbled the sugar lump she held out to him.

As she lifted her saddle on the rack she heard the screech of wheels.

Kevin shouted down the aisle, "Marni! You and Koke won the blue ribbon. Congratulations!"

"Thanks, Kevin. I'm so happy I could burst!"

"Me, too. And I've got wonderful news!"

"Tell me!"

"My dad found us a small house in the country. A bus'll pick me up for school."

"Oh, Kevin, that's great!"

"Marni, would you believe—the new house has a barn! And when Dad heard about me riding alone, he said we could buy Koke!"

A slow flush warmed Marni's cheeks.

Kevin ran on. "Koke is the only horse in the world for me. I think about him every day, and I even dream about him."

Marni couldn't let him continue. "Kevin. . ." she interrupted.

But he was talking so fast he didn't hear. "Jennifer

says my muscles have stretched, and someday I may be able to do everything other people do on horses."

She started to tell him again, but he rushed on. "Koke's going to help me be a rider or a trainer—maybe even an instructor of handicapped kids. Mom will call your parents tonight."

When Kevin finally paused for breath, Marni said in a small voice, "I don't think we can sell Koke to you Kevin. You see. . .we've had another offer."

Kevin's surprise and hurt showed in his eyes. "But Marni, Koke is my whole future. I need him!"

12

THE DECISION

Marni couldn't forget Kevin's reaction when she'd told him about the other offer for Koke. His whole body had sagged, and the happiness had drained out of his face.

Yet Marni's father wanted her to sell Koke to whomever she pleased. Her choice was Captain Blaine. But she kept seeing Kevin looking up at her from his wheelchair pleading, "Koke is my whole future. I need him!"

Tears filled her eyes. It was all very well for Kevin to talk about his needs, but what about hers? If Koke stayed at Riverwoods Riding Center she could see him often. If Kevin bought him, she'd never see her beloved horse again.

Marni felt a cold chill, and her scalp prickled. Kevin was a great kid, a good friend. She'd do anything for him. . . anything but sell him Koke.

When she got home, the phone rang. It was Kevin. "Marni, have you decided?"

"Not yet."

"School's starting. Mom and I have to leave day after tomorrow."

"Well. . .uh. . .I'm thinking about it, Kevin. Say, can you meet me at Riverwoods tomorrow morning? I want to see you before you go." She'd bought Kevin a red cowboy bandanna as a going-away gift.

"Okay, Marni. Mom will drive me there at nine. Can you let me know then?"

"Tomorrow at nine, Kevin. See you."

Marni sat in her rocker for hours, holding her blue ribbon, sorting out her feelings. At daybreak, she dressed and rode to the Riding Center.

She got a whiff of saddle soap and manure as her boots clicked in the quiet barn. Koke whinnied and stamped when he heard her special call.

"Hi, Kokey," she said softly.

He put out his head. Hungry as usual, he gobbled the apple she offered.

Marni reached up and patted his nose. "Kokey, what should I do? If you stay here in the riding school, I can see you every day. It'll be almost the same with us. Maybe some day I can even buy you back.''

Koke's head bobbed as if he understood.

But Kevin's face haunted her again. "Kevin wants you too, boy. He needs you. You'd have a good home and he'll love you very much. . .''

Marni slid open the door and threw her arms around Koke's neck. Tears streamed down her cheeks. "Oh, what should I do?''

Koke drooled apple juice on her jacket. Despite her sadness, she had to smile. She thought about how she and Koke had been inseparable for almost two years. He'd given her self-confidence and helped her to be a better rider. With Koke, her dream of winning a blue ribbon had come true.

Now Kevin needed the courage and self-confidence Koke could give him. He, too, had a dream for the future.

She heard a wheelchair coming down the aisle.

"Marni, are you here?'' It was Kevin.

"Yes,'' she answered.

All at once Marni felt a sensation she'd never had before, the soaring-over-the-rooftops feeling that she'd thought would come from winning a blue ribbon.

Kevin looked tired. "I can only stay a minute. Mom has so much to do. Have you made up your mind?''

"Kevin, I've decided to sell Koke to you."

"Oh, Marni!" He caught her hand and squeezed it. "Are you sure?"

"Yes. I want you to have him."

"I'm selfish for asking you to give him up. But he means so much to me."

"I know you'll be good to Koke, Kevin. You love him as much as I do." Marni didn't feel a bit like a girl who had just given away her most beloved possession. Last June she might have felt differently. But that was long ago. Now she was on top of the world!

"You're the kindest, most generous person I've ever known." Kevin's voice broke, and Marni could feel his happiness.

She rummaged in her pocket for the red bandanna. Then she leaned down, wiped his eyes, and tied it around his neck.

"Go get 'em, John Wayne!"